A staccato hail

The spitting of the submachine gun was followed by a shattering of glass and screams of panic as people scattered on the busy sidewalks.

Trying to regain control of the Jeep, Erika threw a frantic glance behind her. Through the golden hair flapping about her drawn face, she saw Barrabas crouched low in the back, riding with the flow of the vehicle as he yanked the Browning Hi-Power from shoulder leather.

A truck drew up alongside, and from its bed an armed man leaped out, his powerful legs propelling him and landing him cleanly inside the Jeep—right next to the driver's seat.

Although he half turned to the rear, he didn't bring his gun to bear on Barrabas. "Her first," he snarled as he jabbed the weapon at Erika.

SOLDIERS OF BARRABAS

SOLDIERS OF BARRABAS

THE BARRABAS KILL

JACK HILD

A GOLD EAGLE BOOK FROM
WORLDWIDE ®

TORONTO • NEW YORK • LONDON • PARIS
AMSTERDAM • STOCKHOLM • HAMBURG
ATHENS • MILAN • TOKYO • SYDNEY

First edition November 1989

ISBN 0-373-61633-3

Special thanks and acknowledgment to
William Baetz for his contribution to this work.

Printed in U.S.A.

1

The color of the sky over the lake had become a bright gray. A few clouds wafted above, moving quickly and looking like huge puffs of gun smoke.

He wasn't having fun. He didn't know who the four men were who had become his constant companions for the past three days and nights; he suspected they were CIA or a Special Forces contingent working for the Agency. They all seemed to be enjoying themselves immensely. He wished he was still sleeping. He also wished they hadn't taken his gun, a Russian Makarov pistol, away from him. He missed the weapon that had become a part of him since he began the run from Saratov.

"How about that morning air, Val? Bet you don't have fresh air like this back home." The one with the fishing net and shotgun at his feet was grinning at him.

The man who was in control of the outboard motor smirked. He was the least pleasant of the group. "Nah! All that Russkie air stinks."

"Shut up, Sid. Jesus! You can be such an asshole."

They all fell silent, but Sid stubbornly maintained a derisive look on his face.

He didn't like fishing, but it was an important part of their cover. They were supposed to be a group of friendly sportsmen who had come to their Ozark cabin in the late summer to fish, drink beer and get away from the wives. He was wearing a stupid hat that helped hide his features. It was covered with hooks and lures and a big button that read, Fishermen Have the Best Lines. They had stayed sober but had poured a lot of beer down the drain and tossed the bottles out for effect. They were pretending to have a good time, and the four agents talked loudly and used strange American terms like "peckerhead," and Sid's favorite, "well, kiss my balls and call me Charlie!"

Seven nights and eight days to go. The nights were the hardest. He usually dreamed of winter in Moscow and the past triumphs in space. His dreams were always of cold places, as if he longed to be away from the repulsive heat, the dark woods and the buzzing insects. He was starting to sincerely hate the place, and it was becoming harder to appear as if he was actually having fun.

The fishing boat pulled up to the wooden dock where the other two agents were waiting. They carried hunting rifles and wore side arms under their vests. One of them took the rope from the bow and started tying up the boat. "Everything's quiet. There's coffee and chow on in the cabin."

"Blueberry pancakes, hot maple syrup and Canadian bacon," added the other man on the dock, grinning with the kind of pride only a cook has.

He wasn't hungry. Nor was he used to eating a big breakfast, unlike the others, who ate huge meals at every sitting. He had to wonder how they could stay so trim and in such superb condition. He knew their training must be grueling.

He actually felt confident when surrounded by the men. They were obviously some of the best in the world at what they did. He knew he was as safe as he could be, deep in the very heart of America, protected by a crack team of professionals. It would really take a gang of supermen to find him now.

Sid turned off the motor. "Well, let's get Ivan inside and dig in. This fresh air really does something. I'm starved!"

The other guard in the boat gave the one called Sid a stern glare. "His name is Val. That is how you will address him."

Sid shrugged, jumped onto the dock and set off at a quick pace toward the cabin.

The man in the boat with Val sighed and shook his head disgustedly. He gave Val a hand and helped him onto the dock. "Don't pay any attention to Sid. He's a jackass."

They walked toward the cabin, slowly and in the combat-mode formation. He was always surrounded by men with guns. They carried the weapons casually, as if they were of no real concern, but he knew they were tensed and ready for trouble. The professionalism exuding from the men lent him a certain confidence, and it was about the only positive element in his tumultuous life right now.

The morning call of a whippoorwill carried through the soft breeze. It was a peaceful sound, one of the many small things that should be putting him at ease.

He turned to the friendly man walking alongside and gave him a sincere little smile.

The agent smiled back. "Having fun now, Val?"

"It is . . . okay." He shrugged and his smile widened. "Could be much worsened."

"Yeah. It could be worse."

As they approached the cabin, Sid went in ahead of the group. They waited outside, appearing to be preoccupied while Sid gave the safehouse a quick security check.

Sid came back to the doorway and nodded to the group. He was going to tell them it was clear to enter but he could only gargle. His hands went to his throat, as if to feel why he had suddenly lost his voice. The burst larynx was further ruptured by his probing fingers. When he tried to speak again, a bright red stream of blood cascaded down his chin—the results of the 868 mm round that had just torn out his throat.

Silently Sid toppled out of the cabin doorway and dropped onto the dirt. He was dead before he hit the ground.

"Jesus Christ!" the cook exclaimed wildly, cocking his hunting rifle and looking around with desperation.

"Take cover!" shouted the friendly one, turning around to face the woods. He seemed to grunt and the back of his head blew apart, spraying Val with blood and tissue.

"Get down! Get down, Val!"

He was in shock. He felt the hand pulling on his arm. The cook was crouched beside him, trying to pull him down out of the line of fire. What seemed to be mutant insects were buzzing through the air around him. Then he realized they were rounds from the Kalashnikovs. He dropped with the cook, who hit ground just a second earlier.

"Keep your head down, Val."

"Yes!"

He saw the other agent in front of them, crouched with his rifle ready to get off a shot at the snipers if possible. As he watched, the CIA man looked around, searching out the brush, then gasped as he was hit square in his chest. He collapsed onto the dirt and rolled to his left, moaning in pain.

"Hell! Where are those bastards . . ."

The cook was crouched over him, his eyes sweeping the area in a frantic attempt to at least find a target. The morning light was dim through the thick woods, and the early mists were playing tricks. Things that shouldn't move were coming toward them. Phantoms materialized. They were facing a supernatural legion, something unleashed from his darkest nightmare.

The cook lifted his rifle to get off a shot and took a round directly between his eyes. He didn't have time to curse or even to grunt; he died instantly. He simply fell away, his body thumping like a sack of mud as it hit the ground.

Val was alone and defenseless. The death squad was coming at him. He wondered who they were. Was it a KGB or a GRU squad, or a Spetsnaz team sent to retrieve him? Would they kill him or take him alive?

As they finally emerged from the mist they seemed to materialize. They were wearing trebark camo that had made them look as though they were a part of the forest. They carried AK-47s. They wore GSX goggles and full masks, and he couldn't see any human features.

The one in the lead approached the agent rolling in the dirt and moaning in deadly pain. The cries stopped when the demon commando shot him in the head with one AK round.

The entire CIA security team was gone. Val was completely helpless, and still they kept coming, a total of six of them, then seven. His numb brain managed to recollect that Spetsnaz hit teams worked in sevens. So they had caught up to him, after all.

The lead man drew closer, then stood over him like a dominating authority and spoke.

"Hi there, Ivan. Bet we just screwed up your whole day." He definitely wasn't Russian.

There was a roar behind the cabin. He gave a start and looked up. A Blazer 4x4 was tossing rocks and dirt as it slid around the side of the building. Another masked man was at the wheel.

"Our ride is here, pal," said the man standing over him. "Time to hit the road."

So he wasn't going to die. What they had in store for him could be worse. He thought of interrogation...then the gulag. He wondered whether he should beg them to kill him now, cleanly.

"Who are you?" he asked.

"Why, we're the guys who have come to take you away from all this," the man above him said.

"We're your worst nightmare, Ivan," stated the one who was now standing behind the leader.

"Hurry up!" shouted the one in the Blazer. He was nervous and threw quick looks at the surroundings as though he were really expecting trouble any moment.

"Time to go," the leader said, reaching for him.

He gave one soft moan. The hand took his arm, squeezing the triceps, digging into his flesh. He knew it would leave a bruise.

Then he realized the total hopelessness of his situation. He was worried about a bruise when he was certainly going to his death.

2

Walker Jessup had to look twice to recognize the senator. The man approaching his table looked like the familiar lawmaker, an aging diplomat in a wheelchair. But the woman behind him, escorting him through the busy restaurant, was not the usual luscious assistant capable of many services, which included typing at least three words a minute. This woman was a real bowwow.

Jessup leaned his bulk forward in the plush chair and squinted to see better in the dim light. It really was the senator! He was quickly nearing the table, and his wide grin seemed to precede him.

"Hello, Walker." The lawmaker wheeled up to the table and reached for his napkin.

"Senator," Jessup acknowledged. Then he realized he was staring, and turned his head to look at his water glass.

The woman behind the senator checked to make sure he was comfortable. "Will there be anything else, sir?" she asked.

"No, that will be all for now, Mrs. Miskowski. Thank you."

"Shall I mail that correspondence for you now, sir?"

"Yes. That will be fine. Then go home, for heaven's sake. I'll see you in the office in the morning."

"Yes sir. Thank you, sir." She stood straight and turned to leave, almost in a military fashion.

Jessup was staring again. The woman was extremely thin, in her mid-forties and about as homely as possible. She looked like Pee-wee Herman in drag.

As she walked stiff-backed from the restaurant, Jessup pointed after her and asked incredulously, "Who was that?"

"That was Mrs. Miskowski, my new personal assistant," the senator explained. "She's very efficient."

"You gotta be kidding! I mean...well...she's certainly different."

The senator gave a deep, heart-felt sigh as he remembered his previous helper of only the week before. Barbi sported a bouncy backside right out of a sailor's dream. It made the elderly lawmaker want to weep.

"If you think she's bad, you should see my new secretary."

Jessup continued to look extremely puzzled. The senator was a man who appreciated attributes other than professionalism and efficiency in his hired help. He was interested in ladies who could perform admirably with the lights out.

The senator sighed again. "The doctor told me two weeks ago to cut down on some of my more strenuous physical activities. There is evidently a minor flaw in my circulatory system which needs immediate correction."

"No sex?" Jessup was grinning, and there was an evil twinkling in his eyes.

"Well...in moderation..." The senator nearly choked on the words, then lapsed into a miserable silence.

A waiter approached the table and set a plate of food in front of Jessup. Now it was the senator's turn to stare while Jessup inspected his plate with a disbelieving look on his face.

"What the hell is that?" the senator asked, pointing at the plate.

"I took the liberty of ordering while I was waiting for you to arrive. I hope you don't mind."

The waiter handed the senator a menu and left, but the senator was still staring at Jessup's plate. It consisted of a dab of cottage cheese, a couple of celery and carrot sticks, whole wheat crackers and a tiny portion of tuna salad. "Is that an appetizer?" he asked.

"I...am also under a doctor's orders..."

"A diet! Are you on a diet, Jessup? Ha!" The senator displayed the delighted smile of mean-spirited people who prefer to have others share in their suffering.

Jessup was a huge individual who had not acquired his solid mass by eating carefully. In fact, when it came to food, Jessup's very sanity was in question. He loved to eat as much as the senator loved to play with pretty girls.

With a shuddering sigh, Jessup picked up his knife and spread some tuna on a cracker. He looked as if he was going to bawl, and there was a distinct quaver in his voice when he said, "We're getting old, senator."

"Well, it sure as hell beats the alternative!" The senator was now chuckling, his mood completely turned. Misery got its much-desired company.

Jessup munched some tuna. He swallowed and washed it down with a sip of mineral water. His hand was shaking a bit as he reached for more tuna. "I really don't know what you're so worried about, senator. You already proved you have a charmed life."

The senator chuckled again. "It helps to have a little luck on our side in our business, Jessup. But it also doesn't hurt to show a little common sense."

Jessup nodded, thinking about the many times he had worked with this man in the past few years. They could use all the help they could muster in their business. It was certainly no cakewalk out there.

The waiter returned and took the senator's order. When he left, the senator leaned on the table and spoke softly to Jessup. "You probably realize I didn't ask you to come to Washington to talk about old times. There is a little problem . . ."

"There's always a little problem," Jessup commented wryly. He was still in a blue mood.

"We can't get into it here," the senator said. "After dinner we'll go to my office, and I can let you know what I have in mind for you this time."

"Sure."

The senator leaned back in his wheelchair and gave a little laugh. "Meanwhile, let's enjoy our meals here in one of Washington's finest restaurants. The steak I ordered will be magnificent, and the wine is beyond compare...."

"All right! You made your point! By the way, did you see that gorgeous girl over there...to the right, senator. The one with the breathtaking..."

"Truce!" The senator threw up his hands. "Let's just eat and get out of here."

Jessup smiled and tossed down his cottage cheese with an expression of savage consolation.

THE SENATOR WHEELED AROUND to face the couch where Jessup was sitting. He was no longer in a mood even for wicked joviality. "How much do you know about Icefort?"

The senator's question took Jessup by surprise, and he had to think for a moment before answering.

Despite their years of dealing together, the man in the wheelchair could still give Jessup a shock. Just when he thought he couldn't be surprised again, the senator pulled out a whole new bag of tricks.

Walker Jessup was an independent operator, an ex-CIA field director who had left the structure to become a respected free-lancer. Known throughout the inner circles of special warfare and intelligence communities as the Fixer, he had the reputation as a man who could put together any kind of a deal, no matter how dirty or dangerous or secret the request. Jessup could produce results. He knew his way around the shadow lands. He had important and useful contacts at every level of the business, from street informants and petty crooks to the power brokers at Washington's highest echelons.

The senator was a man who took it upon himself on many occasions to become involved in special projects, usually covert operations and involving secret armies in dirty little wars. During the years he had spent in Washington, he had become one of the hidden primary forces within the shadow communities but outside the structured bureaucracy, and had a reputation as a man who could get things done very quietly.

These two men had worked together on a number of projects in the past, each using the other for his own personal gain. They had their hands in many sources of under-the-table funds. Their track record was remarkably good for their type of work, and they consequently had the credentials to afford them power where necessary. They held each other in a wary mutual respect, but in the never-never lands of Washington, trust could only go so far.

Jessup was thinking. He looked at the senator and gave a little shrug. "Icefort is highly confidential information."

"Don't bullshit me, Jessup." The senator's face wore a sneer that looked glued on.

Jessup merely shrugged his massive shoulders again. "Icefort is the code name for a highly secret Soviet space station being constructed in the Taymyr Peninsula, east of Dikson on the Kara Sea. A Big Bird recon satellite has been keeping its eye on the installation where the station is being designed for the past year or so. Data analysts know that the station is strictly military and believe it will be equipped with photon weapons and X-ray lasers. The big worry right now with the eggheads is they don't know how far along with research and development the Soviets really are… And if you want me to put together a penetration team to go into the Arctic Circle, you can forget that!''

The senator held up a hand. ''Don't get your bowels in an uproar, Jessup. It's nothing like that. My interests are in one man, Ilya Valentin, a Russian math prodigy turned weapon designer. His first love is space, and Ilya worked for six years on the Soviets' space-stations program before being transferred into the Icefort Project, as we call it. Ilya has not been a happy man since. He doesn't believe in space-based weapons, and it has been tearing him apart to be involved in their design and construction for the past ten months.''

Jessup grinned and nodded slightly. ''And now Ilya wants to come out.''

The senator grunted. ''Ilya *did* come out. It was a CIA operation.''

''Oh, hell.''

''Yeah. They've already screwed things up royally. Ilya was given some time off from the Taymyr installation to attend a scientific conference in East Berlin. He visited his home in Saratov, packed some belongings and started running. He knew he wouldn't be returning. He had already been in touch with CIA agents.

''Valentin attended the conference for two days and made contact with a CIA sleeper known as Isaac. The agent had everything ready and brought Valentin across on the third day. He was met and guarded by various teams, whisked out of Berlin and flown to San Francisco, and then flown deep inland, to the Ozarks. He was being kept on ice at a highly guarded CIA safehouse, while preparations were being made to give him a new identity and lose him in Washington's scientific community, when the safehouse was hit by a very good squad of paramilitary spooks. The CIA protection team was eliminated, and Ilya Valentin has disappeared.''

"It couldn't get any more dismal," stated Jessup.

"Yep. You got that right. The Agency is in turmoil, working around the clock. They haven't got a clue who snatched Valentin. They think it was a Soviet team; the weapons used were all Russian. It was carried out like a GRU mission. You know Soviet military intelligence favors a kill squad of around eight or nine spooks. But they can't come up with anything concrete . . . and my interests are getting worried.''

"Is it NSA again?" Jessup asked.

"Yes. And, like the Agency, they want Valentin back. But there are others in Wonderland who would just as soon the Soviet scientist stay lost permanently.''

Jessup nodded. "I'll bet. There's a lot of power and money to be made in the race for the militarization of space.''

"You know it," the senator said.

"So, if I understand it correctly, the job here is to find the lost Soviet scientist and bring him back to the United States . . .''

"You got it," the senator replied.

"It's an NSA contract, the basics similar to the ones we negotiated in the past. We have expense money and enough funds to pay the people we need."

The senator nodded.

"Is there background material available?"

"We just happen to have a few loose CIA files on the matter, which I am at liberty to turn over to you if and when you accept the terms of the contract."

Jessup thought in silence for a long moment, then said, "This sounds like something I might be interested in taking."

The senator smiled knowingly. "I thought so."

Jessup chuckled. "And I don't suppose you have anyone in mind to do the fieldwork in this little outing?"

"Do you think... Jessup, do you think you can convince *him* to come aboard?"

"Why don't you say his name, senator? Does it rankle that much?"

"I'd rather eat you know what. But I really think we need Barrabas on this one...."

"There, that wasn't so bad, was it? Yes. This should appeal to Barrabas. He could do it. I'll give him a call."

"Good," said the senator. "I have a suggestion for a starting place. East Berlin and the sleeper. It seems that Isaac may have been blown. A sniper took a shot at him the other day, and he's gone under. The CIA is planning on bringing him out of the cold, but you know how their operations go, slower than elephant shit. While they're screwing around with paperwork and trying to get someone to take the responsibility for the op, your man can go in and have a little chat with Isaac."

"I'll make that suggestion," Jessup said. "But you realize there's no way I can tell Barrabas how to conduct his business. I might as well talk to that chair over there."

"He's a rogue and a scoundrel," the senator responded. "But he's also good at what he does."

"No," Jessup corrected, "not good. Barrabas is the best."

3

Nile Barrabas was sitting in his hotel room in Paris, meditating over a frosty mug of Helden Pils, when the call came through from New York. It was Ducett, Jessup's right-hand man, sounding like he was calling from the moon. There was a terrible crackling on the line.

"Hello...Mr. Sommers..." Sommers was the code name Jessup often used for Barrabas.

"Just a minute," Barrabas said. He set down the phone and picked up the mug, then drained it in a long gulp. He was reflecting on his life, and he didn't particularly care for the result. It was all because of those morons in the bar in Montmartre.

Barrabas had come to Paris for a little R & R. The bars and cafés and nightclubs of the infamous Moulin Rouge strip were a breeding ground for men like him, ex-soldiers and legionnaires who were now members of the brotherhood of *Le Mercenaire*. The charged and often dangerous atmosphere provided the perfect environment for men in the profession to gather and talk and swap lies about their heroic efforts. Barrabas never talked. He would drink good beer and listen and occasionally hint at the reality of the world and their particular line of work.

He was sitting at a bar called Fouguets in Montmartre listening to a tale about drugged ex-patriots in Bangkok fighting to the death like gladiators in a pit. He was nestled between two generations of the breed; on his right, a young kid fresh from his stint in the French army wanting to learn all about Barrabas the legend, and on his left, a washed-up alcoholic ex-merc too drunk to care about anything.

The guy telling the story was a British soldier, a member of a mercenary outfit called The Watchmen. "So they toss old Lucius into the hole to face Chang the Crusher an' Lucius is so stoned by now he thinks he's invincible!"

Barrabas listened politely but thought the story was a bit odd. He had been to Bangkok on a number of occasions, in fact knew the city like the back of his hand, and he never saw anything like the death-fight pits this guy was describing. Just the same, he decided to let the British merc glow in the glory of his tale.

"So Chang grabs Lucius right off and starts to squeeze his head into mash."

The kid next to Barrabas really wasn't interested in learning whether Lucius's skull got squashed. He wanted to know about Barrabas. "Colonel Barrabas...I heard you fought all over. Central America, Angola, Cambodia, Iraq..."

"Don't believe everything you hear," Barrabas advised as he motioned to the waiter for another beer.

"I heard you were the best in the business...I mean you are the best . . . I mean, well . . . everybody told me you were dead."

"That proves my point," Barrabas said. His beer arrived and he paid for it.

" . . . so Lucius doesn't even know he's actually brain-dead and he just keeps on fightin'. He bites Chang's ear clean off and spits it at the crowd."

"So, Colonel, what do you think?" The young soldier was asking the question in all sincerity. "Should I take that job in Scotland?"

Barrabas took a long swallow of the beer, pondering over how to best answer. The drunk merc on the other side of Barrabas squinted at the kid. "Who you talkin' to?"

"Colonel Barrabas."

"Barrabas is dead," the old mercenary said, leaning in front of Barrabas to talk across at the kid. "He was killed in South America. Executed in the Aztec fashion. He was disemboweled an' his innards were stuck on the end of a stick! I was there and saw it all."

"Colonel Barrabas is sitting right here," the kid remarked scornfully as he pointed at Barrabas.

"That's impossible."

"Take a look...who the hell do you think this is?"

The old merc squinted at Barrabas. "Ah! Holy mother of God! A ghost!" The merc jumped to his feet, almost falling over on his back in the process, and announced to the whole room, "Jesus preserve us all! There's a fuckin' spook at my table."

"Excuse me," Barrabas said to the kid. He stood up and reached for the old man's temples, applying pressure to nerves in an aikido move. The drunk merc dropped like a sack of potatoes and fell across the table. Barrabas sat back down.

"That was neat!" the kid exclaimed. "Will you teach me how to do that?"

"No," Barrabas said. "And to answer your first question, you have to let your conscience be your guide." Barrabas hoped he didn't sound like Jiminy Cricket. He liked the kid and really wanted to give him some sound advice. "You have to think long and hard before you go into this business. It's the most stressful and sometimes the most miserable occupation on earth. You'll get all the dirty jobs, the shitty wars that conventional forces can't or won't fight. Your life won't be worth a plug dime. Sometimes your employers will hope you get killed so they won't have to pay you. You'll come up against moral issues all the time. You'll constantly be subjected to the miseries of war, the crying children who saw their parents die and the innocents caught in the cross fire. You should think long and hard before you choose this life-style . . . and for God's sake, don't believe all these stories about the glory of war."

The waiter returned and looked at the old mercenary draped across the table. "Too much to drink," explained Barrabas straight-facedly. The waiter nodded knowingly.

The storyteller was thoroughly absorbed in the details now. "So Lucius has stuff oozing out of his eye sockets, and Chang is really pissed. Blood is squirting about three yards in the air from the hole where his ear used to be . . ."

Barrabas had had enough. He stood up to leave and turned to the kid once more. "Think about what I told you. Think long and hard." Then he left.

Barrabas returned to his room at the Royale Hotel and called room service for more beer. He was still thinking about the speech he had given to the young would-be mercenary. It came from the heart. He had been talking about his own life, about himself.

Barrabas's military career had started when he left his home in Wyoming at age eighteen to enlist in the U.S. Army. He had thought he'd found his purpose. He fit into military life as if he was created to serve, a born soldier. His training had been extensive and when he was ordered to go to Vietnam, he went to serve his country willingly.

As a captain with the 5th Special Forces, Barrabas was allowed to do what he did best—the dirty jungle fighting and special combat missions were his calling. He felt at home in the swamps; the teeming jungles nurtured him, and the constant dangers only built his character. He was happy in this hell, serving the country he respected. He was a true soldier, one of the rare breed of fighting men who came alive in the conflict and thrived on the dangers.

Then came his promotions, all the way to colonel and a cushy desk job with MAC, the Military Attache Liaison Office of MAC, Saigon. He was suddenly taken out of his work and put into the other side of military service, the bureaucracy and political game playing. It was like stuffing a square peg into a round hole. He longed to be back in the action, back with his men whom he could respect and honor in warfare, and away from the paper shufflers and wrench tossers and memo rewriters of the upper echelons of the army. He was forced to watch this social club losing the war and seemingly not giving the least bit of a damn. He was wearied and disgusted.

When Saigon finally fell to the NVA hordes, it felt as though his very soul had been torn out of his body. He clung to the final moment, not willing to give up. He was the last American out of Saigon, fighting to the very bitter end. He left Vietnam behind and left his life in the army, as well.

It was the hardest point in his life. He didn't know what his future could possibly hold. He thought of returning to Wyoming, getting married and maybe starting a family. He could buy a ranch, settle down, build a future. Instead he got very drunk on a regular basis until he understood finally that he needed to live on the edge. Then, what with Jessup going free-lance, he had good connections. The search was over, and what followed was more than a decade as a professional soldier-for-hire. The life-style suited Barrabas in most ways. He became a respected leader, the most desirable soldier for jobs really almost impossible to accomplish. He fought in the jungles and sewers and reeking slums of the world's hot spots. He could definitely say that he had seen it all.

Lately there was a stale taste in his mouth, and he wondered, not without a sense of irony, whether he was starting to experience something akin to a mid-life crisis. Maybe this was how business executives felt when the sales quotas didn't matter anymore. Maybe he should settle down with Erika. He sat in the hotel room in Paris and allowed possibilities to turn over in his mind in a slow progression. For the first time in a long while, he accepted that there could be a future for him, that his life did not necessarily have to stop with the current day.

The phone rang. It was Ducett in New York. "Jessup has another... project. He needs you to report in Washington. Usual channels. ASAP!"

"Right," Barrabas said. After he'd hung up, he stared off into space for a while. Some answers were in various stages of readiness inside him, but the total picture still had to wait. Meanwhile he had to leap into action: he knew it was the better way for him.

Methodically he started to prepare for his departure to Washington. He had the feeling something would meet him head-on.

4

The place reminded Barrabas of past days on football teams. The constant grunting accompanying physical exertion, the smell of male sweat, the thick atmosphere of the type found only in training camps or real gyms. It brought back memories of youth, of days when he had shining dreams and hadn't been on a world tour of Earth's hellholes.

The door opened, and a huge man walked into the little gym. He wore only a pair of training shorts. He was a massive individual with layers of rippled muscles stacked on his torso and limbs. He had put a thin coat of oil on his body so his physique would be accented as he worked out. He exuded vanity.

"Excuse...me..." Walker Jessup was riding a stationary cycle. Sweat beaded his brow, and he was puffing away with the effort. "This...room is... closed. This is a...private session...."

"I gotta train for a contest," the muscle man said, reaching for a set of dumbbells.

Jessup grunted before answering but still tried to look friendly. "I'm sorry...but you really must leave...."

"I got a contest," the man repeated, doing some easy free-curls to warm up his biceps.

There was a pause as Jessup attempted to catch his breath. Meanwhile Barrabas pulled a cigar out of his breast pocket and leaned back to rest against a Nautilus machine.

"Hey! There's no smokin' in here, buddy," explained the bodybuilder. He wasn't the most polite individual Barrabas had ever met, but Barrabas merely shrugged and put the cigar in his mouth.

"Please . . . you really must leave this room," Jessup said, managing to squeeze out the words. His big face was as red as a radish, and his expensive workout suit was soaked with sweat. He sounded terrible. His breathing was strained, and there was an increasingly glazed look in his eyes.

"You gonna make me leave?" the man asked, not even pausing in his routine.

Barrabas walked over to him and placed two strong fingers on his bulging triceps. "Ow! Ow!" The dumbbells dropped on the floor, and Barrabas began gently walking the guy toward the door.

"Ow! Say, fella . . . ow!" The bodybuilder was propelled along in a dancing step in front of Barrabas. He had no control of his actions. "Say . . . ow . . . those are some nice arms you got . . . ow! Did you get 'em pumping iron?"

"No," Barrabas said. "Tossing blockheads." He proceeded to toss the rude man out of the little gym and closed the door.

There was a crash in the adjoining room, and someone cried out, "Shit! Watch what you're doing, dickhead."

Barrabas leaned his big frame against the closed door to prevent any further interruptions. He put the cigar back in his pocket, then looked the Fixer up and down. "Okay, Jessup. So the CIA screwed up another one..."

They were in a place called Powerhouse Gym in Washington. Barrabas had been in town only a few hours, just long enough to get a hotel room and make the initial contact with the Fixer. Jessup had told the merc to meet him at the gym.

Jessup stopped cycling and tried to catch his breath. "Lord! I went in for a physical last week, and the doctor put me on a strict diet-and-exercise program. Said it's vitally necessary for my health. He had me worried, Nile. I vowed I'd follow his advice this time, even if it killed me."

It was hot in the private gym. Barrabas wiped sweat from his brow and ran a hand through his nearly white hair. That was one of the more visible marks left by Vietnam: the others were unseen. He grinned, then started to run in place.

Jessup looked annoyed at the display of energy. "The doctor said he was starting me out easy," he continued in a hurt tone. "I'm supposed to ride this thing two miles every other day."

"How far have you gone so far?" Barrabas asked.

Jessup looked at the odometer on the bike. "An eighth of a mile."

Barrabas ran around in tight little circles, then came to a dead stop before the man mounted on the bike. "Look, Jessup, it's damned hot in here. Let's finish our business so you can do your workout and I can get a cold brew."

Jessup sputtered and wiped sweat away from his eyes. "It really boils down to a simple retrieval mission, Barrabas. My employers want Valentin back. The object of the mission is to find out who snatched him from the safehouse and where he's being held, then get him back. We want him brought directly to Washington, where he can be protected soundly. There will be no more screwing around in the Ozarks."

"What about the CIA?" Barrabas asked. "Will they be out there, getting in my way?"

"Unfortunately, they will have people looking for Valentin as well. But these will be average field agents and investigators. I doubt you will be moving in the same arena."

"Do we have background and research?"

"Yes." Jessup had to chuckle when he thought about the materials the senator had provided. "We have full CIA case files and intel reports. There's a complete research report, dating a year ago, that dealt with setting up a defection. A CIA sleeper agent in place in East Berlin was recruited to pull off the actual job. It has been suggested that this agent could provide a good starting place for your investigation. Apparently he has gone into hiding and is waiting for an Agency team to get him out of the heat. There has been a recent attempt on his life, a very near miss. The sleeper is spooked and went to ground, but it shouldn't be a serious problem to direct you in to have a little chat with this fellow.''

Because Barrabas was silent for a while, his next words took on special emphasis. ''You want me to go into East Berlin . . .''

''Let's just say it has been strongly suggested. But I won't tell you how to do your work.''

''Wise idea,'' Barrabas replied, giving Jessup a hard look.

''Yes, but the East Berlin contact is a strong one. We really believe he has information that can get you onto Valentin's trail.''

''Why hasn't the CIA followed up on this? If the sleeper knows so much, why isn't he spirited away to someplace where he can really talk?''

Jessup chuckled again. ''They're working on it. But it's all bogged down in thick red tape. There are evidently power flexers who are tossing wrenches like crazy. The bureaucratic CIA gears are all jammed, and the Agency is at a standstill while the money-makers and political scavengers fight over the control. Meanwhile the sleeper is holed up in a trap, terrified and praying for help.''

''So if I show up on the scene and offer him that help, you believe we'll have a new recruit who will agree to lead us to Valentin.''

''Well, in a nutshell, it's something like that.''

''Don't kid me, Jessup. It's *exactly* like that. You want me to snatch an agent away from the Agency and put him to work for us.''

"I don't see the problem," Jessup said. "Both the CIA and my employers want the same outcome. They want Valentin found and brought back."

"The problem is that you are going to stick me and my people in the middle of a rivalry between two shadow companies."

"I never knew you cared," Jessup remarked sarcastically. "I mean, you do your job, get paid, then go home...or wherever it is you go. What were you doing in Paris, anyway?"

"Tutoring in warfare."

"What?"

"Never mind. It isn't important."

Barrabas sounded terse, and he also looked somewhat downcast, making Jessup wonder whether there was something wrong. He was a bit disturbed to be seeing the human side of Barrabas. The man had allowed his usual professional demeanor to slip a little. He was exhibiting a quality that came through about as often as Halley's comet.

Jessup decided to ignore all that and go on with business. "I have an agent in West Berlin who will set up your border crossing. You can make contact there, and any intel and supplies can be forwarded ahead. Review the particulars of the mission and let me know what you need to get started. Also give me a budget figure for expenses, and I'll arrange all the funds to be available where and as needed."

"Hold on, Jessup," Barrabas said, looking even more concerned. "I haven't said I'll accept this job."

"What?" Jessup wiped his eyes. "Barrabas, it's perfect for you. A retrieval...help some poor, lonely guy being held hostage. I was sure it would appeal to your way of thinking."

"Thanks, Jessup. I really need your tender words of concern right now."

"Come on, Nile, are you interested in this one or not?"

"No," Barrabas replied. He turned around and opened the door. Before leaving, he turned back and gave Jessup a fleeting look. "Sorry, Jessup. Not this time..."

"Barrabas!"

Barrabas walked out of the gym. The disgruntled muscle man was standing outside the door. Barrabas jerked his thumb towards the gym. "You can go in now."

Barrabas left. The bodybuilder walked back into the gym and looked at a stunned Jessup. "What got into that guy?"

"I wish I knew," Jessup said.

5

Laughter rang out across the room, masking honest emotions. Someone was pretending to be happy. The laughter echoed, and ice cubes tinkling in tall glasses provided a kind of background music to do business by. As Edward Hadley cradled his drink, he considered that when the evening was finally tallied, reality would be measured against impossible hopes.

Someone had once told him that there was more business done and more decisions made at a Washington cocktail party than in all the meetings of Congress and the Senate combined. After years of lobbying and dealing on the inside with Washington's power brokers, Hadley knew that even good, stiff drinks couldn't melt the chill on the inside. There might be more talk, some of it very constructive, but when it came time for action, the red tape was still very tangled. Senators became sober, congressmen had hangovers and moods changed. The morning after always brought business as usual.

Edward Hadley walked through the crowd of revelers, sipping his diet soda. He passed by all the regulars, the political administrators, influential politicians and embassy people. Money was talking as usual, and the dealers were listening. Many wore smiles but exuded hate. Hadley gave off a real smile, amused by the game.

He was looking for another like himself, a man who didn't belong. He found him in a corner, talking with a group of power dealers. Hadley smiled again when he saw that it was the right group.

He knew that the man he was looking for went by the name of Jerry. He was easy to spot from across the room; he was the one who wasn't casting a shadow. Hadley wondered whether a mirror held up in front of Jerry would show a reflection. He thought it might be too disturbing to find out.

Hadley was about to head across the crowded room toward Jerry when a senator from Utah grabbed his arm. "Edward! How have you been? You haven't been in Washington for a while. How's Mary and the kids?"

"Yes. Hello, Senator. I've been busy. The family is fine...."

"Good. Good." The senator really didn't care about Hadley's life or his family. He was primarily concerned with Hadley's money.

Edward Hadley was a self-made man. He had started his personal quest just twenty years before as a real estate investor. He used his profits to start a business, then another, becoming an ambitious entrepreneur. When the profits increased, he bought businesses and reaped handsome rewards. The money grew, and he tried to keep a low profile but his lifestyle wouldn't allow it. He began going to Washington, and what he observed there made him nauseated. There was double-dealing, lying and cheating. The important issues were pushed aside. Nothing was getting done. He had wanted to become involved, to help in a positive and constructive way, but nothing positive or constructive was in the works.

Then he found out what was happening in the shadows. He met Jerry and a few others like him, and Edward Hadley found a way to get involved in the things that could make a difference. He got into the secret deals. He began talking in whispers. He slid out of the bureaucracy and into the cold world of dark things that didn't really happen. And he began making a difference.

"I was wondering, Edward," remarked the senator from Utah. "Have you had the opportunity to review that bill I'm trying to get passed?"

"Yes." But Hadley wasn't paying much attention: he was looking steadily at Jerry.

"Fine. Fine. I'm glad." The senator really wasn't glad that Hadley had reviewed his bill, nor did he care what Hadley thought about anything. The senator was now getting to the only issue he really cared about. "This little project could really use some additional financing, Edward. There never seems to be enough—"

"That's fine, Senator. Contact my office in the morning, and I'm sure we'll manage something."

"Well...that's wonderful, Edward! I can always count on you."

"You must excuse me, senator..."

"Of course." Now that the senator had what he wanted, he was more than happy to excuse Hadley.

His next order of business was the blond assistant to a Nevada congressman who was eager to prove herself in the important circles of Washington. The senator wanted to help her. "You have a nice stay in Washington, Edward. And I'll call in the morning...."

"Yes. Good."

The senator walked away, heading for the blonde. Hadley continued his trek across the fantasyland of the cocktail party toward Jerry. He kept low, hoping he wouldn't be disturbed again.

He wasn't. He approached the group that included Jerry. As he walked up to them, he could hear the conversation. It was exactly what he was hoping for.

"I seriously discouraged this project. Bringing out a defector is always dangerous. You know, it's scandal time, and we really can't afford another stir."

"Not only that," said another Washington insider. "You know as well as I do that there's a lot of money being gambled on the militarization of space. A wild card like the Russian could seriously screw up some research and development funding. We need to keep our people in business."

"To say nothing of our... I mean *the* plans for the industrialization of space," another wheeler-dealer added. "There are American interests at stake—business and industry. No, I must strongly agree with you gentlemen. Our visitor from Russia should be left at large."

"How is the Agency taking this?" a bureaucrat asked.

"As well as can be expected," a dealer answered. "It was their project, after all. Christ! Sometimes I think those ambitious glee-club boys need a leash. They get a wild hair up their ass over there, and it takes a top executive to put a stop to their nonsense."

"A bunch of damned crusaders!" added one power broker.

Hadley decided he had heard enough. He approached the group. "Gentlemen."

A dealer turned to him and pretended to smile. He had sensed money approaching. "Oh, hello, Edward. How are Mary and the kids?"

"Family is fine. Everything is peachy. Now, if you'll excuse me..." Hadley put a hand on the power dealer's chest and gave him a firm shove out of the way. "Jerry! How about a game?"

"Hello, Ed," said the gray man standing at the center of the group. "I just had a game, but I'm up for another."

"Good."

The two men left the group and headed in the direction of the billiards room. When they maneuvered through the clusters of people successfully, they entered and closed the door behind them.

Jerry took a deep breath. "What a bunch of grade A idiots!"

"Yeah. It makes me want to heave," Hadley said, giving his head a shake to accent his disgust.

"Money. Power. Personal gain. It's all those bastards care about."

"I know."

There was a silence while the two men pondered the evils of Washington. After a while, when their mood became as dark and thick as chimney smoke, Jerry gave a little grunt and said, "I suppose we should pretend to have a game."

"Yeah. Eight-ball okay?" Hadley asked. Jerry gave him a little nod. "I'll rack."

They approached one of the tables and went through the motions of having a game. Hadley racked the balls, and Jerry prepared to break.

"Is there any progress on your end?" Hadley inquired, reaching for the chalk.

"I'm afraid the news isn't good, Ed." Jerry gave the balls a solid break.

"What's wrong? You put the Fixer on it, didn't you?"

Jerry was NSA, and was one of the president's specially enlisted advisors. The President himself wanted this one to be a success. He believed in the Star Wars program, the dream of having guardians in space that would make nuclear war obsolete. It would have to be a joint effort, but Russia wasn't cooperating. An ace in the hole like Ilya Valentin was an important element in his plans to advance the overall program.

Jerry lined up a shot and gave a solid stroke. The three ball dropped. "I'm afraid there has been a little problem. The Fixer's SOF team leader turned it down."

"Shit."

"Yeah. My sentiments exactly. How about your group? Is there any chance the committee can become involved?"

Edward Hadley was a member of a shadow club known only as "the committee." It consisted of powerful and extremely wealthy citizens who had decided they were tired of sitting on the sidelines while the Washington power brokers screwed things up. They had put their resources into joint actions, maintaining their own brand of justice in world matters. They operated by the cowboy mentality; damn the law...let's just get the job done! Their primary concern—about the only constant in the matters they had taken on—was that the situations they created should benefit the members of the committee. They were not stupid people, but sometimes they let their power go to their collective heads.

Hadley sighed. "I'm afraid we're in the same boat, Jerry. Without a Special Operations Force to take this thing on in the field, all we can do is sit around and talk about it."

Jerry missed his next shot. "Yeah. I wonder just what went wrong? The Fixer has always been able to put together a mission on a minute's notice in the past. He's bogged down on this one, trying to recruit a man to lead the retrieval team."

Hadley approached the pool table to take his turn. He spent a lot of time chalking his stick, obviously deep in thought. "I wonder if the Fixer has lost his edge. Maybe we should contact the senator and discuss an alternate plan. It might be time to contract a new projects director."

"Damn!" Jerry said, leaning on his cue. "I really hope that isn't the case. Things have gone so well the past few years. With the Fixer, we've been able to keep it all deep in the hush. There have been almost no mistakes.''

"Things change, Jerry. Men go through changes…"

"Yeah, okay. But let's give him a little more time to try to put it together."

Hadley shot so hard he sent a ball flying from the table. It hit the polished wood floor with a thump and rolled toward the center of the billiards room. "So we sit and we wait … and we wonder what the hell went wrong."

Jerry leaned on the pool table and stared at Edward Hadley. "Yes. We wonder. The big question is, where is Ilya Valentin?"

6

Ilya Valentin was in the lap of luxury.

His prison cell was spacious and lavish. The bed was massive and extremely comfortable, and he had spent a good deal of his time there catching up on his sleep. The floor was covered with a thick, plush carpet. The furnishings were obviously expensive and designed for comfort. Nevertheless, the room was a prison. The door was always kept locked, and there were bars on the windows.

He had no clear idea when he had been taken captive at the cabin. He was given chloroform, and a hood was slipped over his head. He went to sleep in that nightmare, and when he woke, he was in a Gothic dream.

He looked out the window on the west side of his prison and saw rolling hills and green meadows. He was in the country. He had seen horses grazing and had heard geese honking that morning as they flew by.

When lunch was delivered by the pretty servant girl, he saw the man with the gun in his usual post just outside the door. The meal was good, as they all were, consisting of roast hen, sweet potatoes, wild rice and rich coffee. When he had finished the meal, the girl again materialized, as if by magic, and took the remains away. The gunman was still at his door, and that was intimidating.

But he knew that the real magic was technology. A closed-circuit camera watched him relentlessly from high in one corner of his room. The angle at which the camera was mounted allowed him to be viewed at every spot in the room. There was a second camera in the bathroom. He had absolutely no privacy.

He was not in Russia, of that he felt certain. The people who were keeping him were not Soviets. Those he had met were an odd mix of European, American and British. His kidnapping seemed to be an international effort.

He sat at the desk. He had been provided with scientific journals and books to read. He had paper and pens and a portable computer to keep him busy, and he would not be bored. It was obvious his keepers wanted to make him happy. He was actually living better than he had ever lived before. Even his captivity was easy to take, because in a way he had never been a truly free man. At most he had been a worker for the good of Mother Russia. As a man who had enjoyed few real pleasures in his lifetime, he decided it was a good time to reflect on his self-pity and create a maudlin mood.

He figured that maybe he had been in his luxurious prison for three days. This was his fourth. He had slept most of the first three, and he had to admit he felt physically good. He was rested and well fed. He was more than comfortable and had everything he could ask for to become involved in interesting work and study. Still, he felt it only proper that he should feel sorry for himself.

He was sitting at the desk, thumbing through the latest issue of *Scientific American*, when the door opened once more, and a tall, stately man entered the room. He was well dressed in an exquisitely tailored suit. His silver hair was meticulously styled, and the few lines he had allowed to etch his features made it tough to guess his age. He looked to be in his mid-forties, but Valentin guessed that was off by at least a decade.

When the man spoke, he did not sound like an American to Valentin's ears. "Professor Valentin. How are you?"

"I am well, but why am I here?"

"First things first, Professor. And how have you been treated?"

"I have been treated well."

"Good. Good. I have instructed my people to afford you every courtesy." The stately gentleman closed the door behind him and walked into the center of the room. The armed guard in the hall outside was keeping a very watchful eye on everything, trying to impress his boss.

"You are certain that you are comfortable, Professor?"

"Yes. I am well." He decided to press on. "Where am I?"

"You are at my estate."

That wasn't a lot of information. He tried again. "Who are you?"

"I'm a friend of your homeland. I have decided that you will be a very nice gift."

"I do not understand. I will be gift?"

The man chuckled. "That's right. I have a conference to attend in Moscow in ten days, and I have decided to take you along. I shall return you to where you belong so you may continue your important work on Icefort."

"No! That will not happen! I will go to gulag!"

"Professor, no need to have such a negative attitude. It will certainly be up to our friends what fate is in store for you, but be confident, my dear fellow. You are an important asset to the cause. You can still assist in the development of the fortress in space... though I doubt you will ever be allowed to attend another conference."

"I have no hope if you return me. You must understand. You will be taking me to my doom."

"I doubt that. You're just too important to the Icefort Project. You are needed, Professor. You are a very valuable man, and we cannot afford to lose you again."

"I do not know this Icefort..."

"It's what the Westerners call it. The space station, sir. Your work for the past year. You certainly remember your precious work?"

"Yes." He didn't know what else to say, so he sat in silence.

The tall man walked around him. He was grinning, and there was an air of malice about him, as if all his wealth and power were obtained through catering to the devil. Of course, Valentin thought, if he was in league with Moscow, that was not far from the truth.

There was a long, pregnant moment of uncomfortable silence while the man sized Valentin up. It dawned on the scientist that his captor was looking over stock. The hapless professor was nothing more than a valuable item to be traded. What had the man called him, a gift? Now he really had something to be morose about.

"I...am going to Moscow with you next week..."

"That is correct. Until then, you will be kept here. If there is anything you want, or need, just ask. I wish to provide you with the essentials for you to continue your work while you are staying with me."

"I...understand."

"Good." The man stood close to Valentin and placed a hand on his shoulder. He gave a squeeze. "Escape is impossible. Your situation, the security here, is watertight. The best thing for you to do is resign yourself to the fact that you are going home and continue your work. You will be happiest if you put your mind, and yourself, to constructive purposes. Do you understand what I am telling you?"

"Yes."

"Good." He gave Valentin's shoulder another strong squeeze and turned to leave the room. "One more thing. I don't want to dirty my hands by killing you, but if you attempt anything foolish, my people have been instructed not to hesitate. You are valuable property to me, but to them, you are shit."

The man left the prison cell, closing the door solidly behind him. Valentin heard it being locked.

The hopelessness set in. A black mood swept through him like a sudden sickness. He put his face down on the desk, resting his forehead on folded hands, and began to weep quietly.

There was one man who could still help him from the outside. He had made one friend through all his ordeal. That was Isaac, the agent in Berlin who had been responsible for getting Valentin to the United States. He had been in charge of the math professor's welfare.

Now Professor Ilya Valentin needed help. He needed a friend. Was Isaac still out there? Would he be in charge of the hunt for the lost Soviet scientist? Would he have a team of hard, tough professional men searching for him? Valentin had to count on something, on somebody. It might as well be Isaac.

Ilya Valentin forced back a sob. He now had something to cling to. Then he did something his friend had taught him during their hideous, desperate run through Germany. Professor Ilya Valentin prayed.

7

He felt like a rat that had been trapped in a hole and forgotten.

The agent known as Isaac took the pot of freshly brewed coffee off the burner and carried it to the wooden table in the middle of the room. He poured himself a mug and put the pot back on the hot plate to keep it warm. Hoping to ward off sleep, he sat down and sipped the strong brew, again wondering where the hell help was.

They were supposed to have him out by now. The master plan had called for his retreat right after the professor was delivered safely to the West. But it had gone all wrong. He was waiting to be taken out when the sniper tried for him, smashing the window of his apartment and making the pillow on the couch next to his face disintegrate. It had been the most terrifying incident in a string of horrors. He had gone to ground, hiding in this awful place, afraid to even go too near the window.

Isaac had lived with fear all his life. He had been born and raised in tyranny, a citizen of East Berlin from his birth. He knew little joy in life, at least not like those he later encountered in school. He was allowed to attend university in the West, and it was there that the Central Intelligence Agency had recruited him.

They told him he could help others like himself. He could join their dedicated and well-justified fight against the tyranny of the Soviets. He could help innocent and good people like his parents, now dead, who had never really experienced true freedom. He could help, and then he could live a fine life in the United States of America, safe and free from his sad past.

The recruiter had been a smooth talker. The man now known as Isaac had willingly given himself over to the cause. He had been eased into the underground network of espionage and brought to Langley for training. Six months in classes on the dark arts of intelligence warfare followed, and the confusions began to churn in his mind. The Agency psychologists had a go at him and did their devious job well, and at the end of his grueling training period, the man known as Isaac was ready, willing and able to serve in the strange world of covert actions.

He became a sleeper. He was placed back in East Berlin, a degree in liberal arts in hand, and he had been told to go about daily life, making a living, become part of the society and wait. When they needed him, they would call.

It had been four years. He had taken a job at a bookbinders, found a rather nice apartment and went about his life. He seemed to be just another good citizen, doing his part to make the society work. He would walk the streets, to and from his job, and dine out at night, seemingly alone and a bit forlorn. There was nothing special about this man, on the outside. On the other side, his CIA training was at constant work. He was looking for escape routes, safehouses, people he could trust and count on when things started to happen.

He waited and worked, and it wasn't as easy as he had thought it would be. He knew he could be called at any time. The Agency hadn't spent time and money on his training to forget about him. Then finally it happened, and without much warning. A man came to his apartment one evening and told him about a Soviet scientist who was attending a conference in a few weeks. The scientist wanted to defect. It was time for Isaac to awaken and do what he had been trained for: he was to bring the man out, get him across the border and safely into the hands of a team of field agents. Then Isaac was to go through one more brief delay, the faceless man had promised, and he would be brought out of the cold. He would be given a hero's reception in the U.S. He would have the life he had always wanted.

Isaac had done his job well. Throughout the days and nights of acute tension, easing Ilya Valentin out of the guarded conference, holding him until the way was clear and the retrieval team was in place on the other side…the nights of waiting, while police searched the streets. Then that unforgettable night when they finally made the desperate run to the border. Ilya had shaved his beard and wore the clothes of a worker. His papers were in order—another service provided by Isaac. There should not have been anything to worry about; the armed guards at the border were always there. The KGB had not arrived in East Berlin yet. It was the perfect time for the crossing, and it went without a hitch. Isaac returned to the shadows to wait for his turn.

Then it went wrong. He received the message that the scientist had been taken from the bodyguards. Isaac may be needed to assist in the hunt. He would be brought out sooner than anticipated.

His hopes soared. He had liked Ilya, had made a friend of the poor, scared scientist, and he wanted to help in the search. But mostly, he wanted to be a free man!

The message had been special delivery, probably through an Agency courier. It had also been the last contact he had from them.

The assassin had burst the bubble of his dream. The near-miss sent Isaac into hiding, and the ratty little hole of an apartment—a place he had found during his sleeping duty—had become his reality. Every spy needs a hiding place, somewhere to go when plans fail to work out. Isaac had his hideout, a little place to dwell in terror and wait for a miracle.

He finished the coffee and got up to pour another cup. His hand was shaking. He couldn't pour. Thinking about it always made it seem worse, if that was possible. Isaac sat back down in the creaky chair and put his face in his trembling hands.

He had taught Ilya how to pray. He had tried to give the scientist some inner peace during the days of the run. Now he would take his own advice. He prayed again, for someone to help. He now realized that he couldn't count on the Agency. Things were too wrong. They had obviously abandoned him. He was alone... yet he needed someone.

8

The sounds of Amsterdam ceased to exist when Erika entered the room. In fact, everything in Barrabas's world would stop as if suspended in another dimension whenever Erika Dykstra was around.

She was as stunning to Barrabas as she had been the very first time he had seen her, so many lifetimes ago, in Vietnam, on the beach in Vung Tau. Tall, blond and radiant, Erika was the one woman who drew Barrabas back to her, even if the absences became longer and more frequent. If there would ever be a permanent woman in Barrabas's world, it would be Erika. He had tried in the past, wanting to have his cake and eat it, too. Erika and his work were opposing poles of experience complicating his life....

"Are you ready, Nile?"

He took a deep breath and let it out audibly. "Yes..."

"Good heavens, Nile! Don't sound so morose. We're just going out for dinner. What's the matter with you, anyway? Are you sure you're not on a mission?"

"No. No mission."

"Well, then cheer up a bit. We're going to have a nice night on the town."

"Sure."

She fell silent then, but restlessly reminded herself that Barrabas had been acting strangely. It bothered her. Nile Barrabas was never what could be called the life of the party, but when he was with Erika, he was usually as close to cheerful as he got.

But not this time. Barrabas seemed moody, as if he was in deep thought, pondering something that was obviously very disturbing for him. He had arrived at Erika's apartment in Amsterdam the previous afternoon quite unexpectedly, which was usually the way with Barrabas. They had their usual passionate greeting, a long night of love, followed by a leisurely day of relaxation and intermittent pleasures.

Something was bothering Barrabas. Erika could sense it, feel it in his aura. They had been lovers for too many years, through too many varied experiences, for Barrabas to hide his emotions from her. She had become a part of him, something more than just a woman to amuse him between jobs, though that was how she often felt. But those feelings would never last, and the true feelings would always return. This time was no exception. Erika knew how she felt...but it was Barrabas who was different. Something wasn't quite right.

His mood had grown darker, more forboding. He seemed to be lost in private thoughts and actually hiding something from her. He told her he was going to talk about it over dinner and indicated he wanted to ask her something.

She wondered whether he was going to pop the big question. He knew how she felt about his work, the missions to godawful places with no names. The days and long nights of waiting while he was out there, with his much-valued team, maybe never coming back. There were only five of them left. Barrabas and his SOBs. At times in the past, she had demanded that he decide... them or her.

He had never been willing to make that decision, to make a certain commitment. And she herself knew it wasn't fair to give him that choice between his work or her, but there was only so much waiting and wondering she could take. She couldn't just stay at home, anticipating the day he wouldn't return.... She just couldn't live forever like that.

Erika and her family were in the moving business. They moved rare commodities such as art, jewels and gold, through a seasoned network, all tax and duty free. Business was always good for Netherlands Imports Management, and had been profitable for five Dykstra generations. Barrabas was welcome to join Erika. His life wouldn't consist of sitting around on his thumbs. There was danger in the moving business—border crossings, piracy, thieves and smugglers to contend with. Nile Barrabas would be a welcomed addition to the Dykstra business. He could be with the woman he loved, and the job wouldn't be a run-of-the-mill time-waster, either.

But it just wasn't soldiering, and Barrabas was a soldier. He was at his best when living on the edge. He seriously wondered whether he could be happy in any other life-style. Despite hating what war could do to men, he needed to be one of the brotherhood of fighters, a member of a legion, a soldier.

His feelings were suddenly very mixed and confusing. He thrived on the things he hated. He had never examined things so much before. He usually hadn't stopped to ponder the painful side for too long. He had always done his job, and done it well. He approached his work from a cold and hard standpoint, realizing fully that it was a part of him, yet keeping the real involvements at arm's length. The grief and misery and loss were just the underside of his chosen profession.

But something had given him pause, and now his conscience, which had always been there, keeping his work in line, was getting the best of him. He lived and worked by a code, his own code of fairness and justice. He was proud of his record, his achievements in the worlds of special warfare. He had become the best at it, and consequently, he had made himself wealthy. He could afford to retire. He loved Erika and wanted her more than any other woman. He knew that sometimes it was best that men changed before they burned out, before the work became drudgery and they began making mistakes. Mistakes in Barrabas's business would mean death . . . for his team as well as himself. He could not afford to stay in the business if he had lost the edge!

They left Erika's apartment building and walked down the narrow street running parallel to the canals. The tender glow of twilight made the trimmed gardens and shrubs at the waterside look especially lovely. It was a soft, romantic night, and snatches of music floated by occasionally on the mild and scented air. Erika was smiling with anticipation and Barrabas looked absentminded but less grim than earlier. Both of them were too wrapped up in their own thoughts and emotions to notice the boat slowly following them down the canal.

They entered the garage at the end of the street where Erika kept her vehicles. She showed the pass to the young attendant and went inside to get her new Jeep.

"Do you like it, Nile?" she asked as they were climbing in.

"Nice." Barrabas got behind the wheel and drove out of the garage and onto the narrow road. It was while he waited for the traffic to clear to make his turn toward the center of the city that he saw them.

There were two of them, standing beside an S-10 pickup truck parked along the curb with its motor running. They were in full gear, wearing tiger-stripe jackets with the hoods up, GSX goggles and full face masks. They were probably harmless, kids playing their games, but Barrabas kept an eye on them.

Erika saw them also. "Who are those guys?" she asked.

"Wargamers."

"What?"

"Guys dressed up for action pursuit games. They shoot paint balls at one another and play war. It's really caught on and become an international sport."

"Maybe you should take it up instead of those real games you play, Nile," Erika suggested with a smirk.

"Sure."

Barrabas noticed that there was a third man inside the truck, keeping the engine running. It was impossible to tell whether they were watching the Jeep because of the hoods and gear, but as Barrabas pulled out into the stream of traffic, the two who were standing jumped in the back of the S-10, and the vehicle began to follow.

Then Barrabas's instincts took over. This was going to be trouble, and a subtle but pervasive change came over him.

Erika noticed it also. Barrabas seemed to grow stronger and more alert, as if something inside him had come alive and was snarling, flexing its muscles, preparing for the fight. He was being transformed, becoming one with his purpose, a whole warrior.

Erika looked at him as if she were seeing a man change into a werewolf right before her eyes. She had seen the transformation before, but it always scared her.

"Oh-oh..." She had turned around and gotten a look at the truck. The two riding in the bed were reaching into Army cargo sacks. The S-10 was gaining on the Jeep, driving rudely through the night traffic. She felt Barrabas speeding up to try to maintain a safe distance between the two vehicles yet not wanting to endanger the others on the narrow street.

Erika looked at Barrabas, and he saw panic starting to show on her lovely features. "Dammit, Nile! Are you sure you're not on a mission?"

"No mission."

"Well, then, who the hell are these guys?"

"Beats me."

Erika realized that she should let him deal with the situation at hand without interruption from her. No matter what the reason, they were in some sort of danger, and he was an expert in that kind of situation. Erika could almost see the wheels turning inside his soldier's brain, calculating the logistics of the fight to come, figuring how to keep bystanders from getting caught in the cross fire and how to take the pursuers out as quickly and efficiently as possible.

Life with Barrabas would just never change, she thought resignedly. She opened her eyes and turned her head to look fleetingly at the approaching truck. It was gaining on the Jeep, pulling up beside them. The two clowns in the back were wielding Uzi submachine guns.

Erika gasped and reached out to touch Barrabas's arm. "They have automatic weapons!"

The truck swerved and hit the Jeep with a solid thump. "Ah! My Jeep!" Erika clutched at the dashboard as they were hit again.

"Take it, Erika!" commanded Barrabas, and pulled her toward the wheel while he pushed himself backward and began to climb into the back of the Jeep.

She grabbed the wheel and fought furiously to keep the vehicle on the street. As Barrabas vacated the seat and jumped into the back, Erika slid over to replace him. The Jeep swerved slightly in the process, hitting the truck and throwing the two men in the bed off balance.

"Nice move!" Barrabas said.

They were entering Amsterdam's Walletjes district, where the streets became even narrower and were filled with roving night people. The twilight became a shower of neon lights, giving the chase an eerie quality, as if they were racing into a techno-hell. Night was falling fast.

Erika heard the staccato of an Uzi being discharged. There was the tinkling sound of glass breaking and screams of desperate and sudden panic from the sidewalk on her right. Stray shots from the Uzis were causing havoc on the street!

Barrabas was crouched in the rear of the Jeep. He gained his balance, letting his full weight be taken by the strong muscles in his powerful thighs. He was riding with the flow of the vehicle, looking like a kid on a ride at a carnival. He reached inside his dinner jacket and withdrew the Browning Hi-Power from its shoulder harness.

There was another burst from an Uzi. The men in the truck were off balance. Their driver was giving priority to the chase rather than keeping the vehicle steady so the gunmen could do their jobs.

Barrabas held on to the back of the passenger seat with one hand and concentrated on taking steady aim into the cab of the truck. He rode with a bump, the muscles in his legs taking the slight shock like coiled springs, then fired. He got off two shots, clean head shots. The driver gasped as he tried to reach for his shattered skull, and then died. His body slumped across the seat, disappearing from sight.

Now there was nobody driving the S-10, and the driverless truck raced crazily down the crowded street. The truck hit a bump and began to career wildly. It swerved over and struck the Jeep one last time, veered right and drove onto the sidewalk.

A small group of people scattered in sudden desperation. The truck had broken up a drug transaction, and the dealer cursed as he dropped his goods only moments before they were crushed by a tire.

One of the men in the rear of the truck screamed under his face gear and collapsed. The other leaped, his strong legs taking him out in a high, straight dive. He flew through the air, carried by the laws of physics and the momentum of the speeding vehicle he had just vacated. He twisted like a cat, and just before he landed cleanly inside the Jeep next to Erika, Barrabas couldn't help but give him credit. The guy was good, and he was going to be tough to take out.

The S-10 made one final run. It cut directly across the sidewalk and smashed into what appeared to be a house of ill repute. Huge glass windows exploded with a crashing sound, and the girls who were selling themselves in the windows like merchandise in a department store screamed and leaped out of the way. The truck plowed into the building, turned sideways and rolled, sealing the fate of the man crouched in the back.

Barrabas considered that now there were two down and one to go. But that one was hunkering in the seat next to Erika, getting his balance and about to shoot her with an Uzi. Barrabas launched himself into action.

He grabbed the man's hood and face mask. He gave a mighty pull, tearing off the gear and letting it fall into the Jeep. The man cursed and turned toward

Barrabas but tried to blast Erika first. The Uzi discharged, but the rounds went high when Erika ducked. Somehow she managed to keep control of the speeding vehicle, and Barrabas registered a sense of pride in her ability to keep her cool.

Barrabas clutched the killer by his tiger-stripe jacket and gave another pull. The man came over the seat and tumbled into the back. Erika began slowing down, cautiously applying the brakes so Barrabas wouldn't be put off balance. The killer was trying to get up, clawing at Barrabas, ready for a fight. He had lost the Uzi, but he had a knife, a recon Tanto in its sheath, strapped to his leg. The man was actually snarling at Barrabas, his eyes full of fury, and he looked as if he was gearing up for hand-to-hand combat.

Barrabas let the man spring up at him then knocked him back down by means of an elbow to the nose. It broke with a popping sound and a blossoming of blood. The man cursed and dropped onto his rump.

Barrabas picked up the Browning from where he had placed it. The man was up and at him again, despite the tremendous pain in his face. He smoothly drew the vicious survival knife from its sheath and swept it toward Barrabas's eyes, trying for a cut that would blind and put the merc at an immediate disadvantage in the fight. It didn't work. Barrabas effortlessly dodged the swipe, raised the handgun and shot the killer in the forehead. The attacker died instantly.

"That's that," Barrabas stated, putting the Browning back into its holster and moving forward to check on Erika.

She had the Jeep under control and was pulling it to the curb. The vehicle came to a complete stop, and Barrabas climbed into the seat next to her. He saw that with the immediate danger over, a delayed reaction was setting in. Fine tremors shook her body. "Nice going. You did good."

Erika had trouble getting the words out. "What was that for? Any idea, Nile?"

"Not a clue, really. But in my line of work..." he said, allowing the words to trail off. Erika would know that in his line of work enemies sometimes came back to haunt you.

"They're certainly not my friends," Barrabas added in mock explanation, and Erika gave off a shuddering sigh. The lights of Amsterdam's red-light district were reflecting off them like a neon-red bloodbath. People were gathering in groups, looking around furtively and pointing, talking about the sudden violence they had just witnessed. In the distance, a police siren sounded like the banshee of lost souls, coming to claim its prize. But Barrabas was not going to wait for an encounter with the law. "Let's put this behind us for now," he remarked. She nodded in agreement, and the Jeep took off.

BARRABAS EXAMINED the face gear he had salvaged from the street battle. Inside the mask was a tag reading, Bay Team-7.

It was the major's work, then, Barrabas knew. He had sent a seventh-class squad of assassins after him. Barrabas pondered what it could mean. He couldn't arrive at a solid reason for—plain enmity aside—the timing of the attack. But one thing he knew for certain: he had to go into action, almost any action, to release his revved-up energies.

Erika came back into the room and handed Barrabas a beer. She took a good swallow of her own double scotch on the rocks. She was still shaking.

They were back in Erika's apartment. Dinner had been forgotten. Erika was too upset and Barrabas was too charged with adrenaline to be hungry.

They sat in silence for a long while, both lost in thought. Then Erika sighed loudly and asked, "Nile? Wasn't there something you wanted to ask me?"

Barrabas looked up at her, only half-hearing the question. "Huh? Oh . . . yeah. Can I use your phone? I need to call Jessup."

"Well, excuse me!" Erika stood up and left the room in a huff.

Barrabas picked up the phone and called New York. He continued staring at the face mask as he waited for the lines to connect. He knew the battle was a bad sign; his cover had been blown even before he had started the mission. Well, that would just make it more interesting, Barrabas thought, and then he heard the Fixer answer the phone.

"Jessup. It's Barrabas. I'm ready to retrieve that package we talked about a few days ago."

"Barrabas! Where are you?"

"Amsterdam."

"Uh, with Erika?"

"Yes. Now I'm ready to start the job. Contact the people in Washington and get a contract drawn. I'm going to start pulling the team together. I think a few of the SOBs are available to start immediately."

"Hold it a minute, Barrabas..."

"I'll set up a rendezvous in West Berlin in two days. Contact your agent there and tell him we're coming and to set up a border crossing. I want to have that chat with Isaac."

"Wait...Barrabas. I actually have someone else lined up..." Jessup paused, then continued in a petulant voice. "You did turn me down, remember?"

"Well, so who do you have in mind?"

"Carter."

"Either you were getting desperate, or you don't mean it at all," Barrabas snorted. "Own up, Jessup."

"I do have something else for you, Nile. A grocery store with security problems..."

"Shove it, Jessup. Just do what I told you. I'm on this one, like it or not. Give the greengrocers to Carter and get this one fixed."

"Now, why should I let some burned-out mercenary handle a job like this?" Jessup chortled, obviously enjoying himself at Barrabas's expense.

Suddenly, things turned serious, and Jessup's faith in Barrabas was totally renewed. "I have an idea about who snatched Valentin," Barrabas stated.

"You do? Are you sure?"

"Come on, Jessup. Would I kid you?"

It was a ridiculous question. "Who did it, Nile?"

Barrabas chuckled to himself so Jessup wouldn't hear. "I have to check a few things out, Jessup. While I'm doing that, you get things set up in West Berlin. I'll be there in two days."

"Where are you going now?" Jessup asked.

"Paris."

"Paris—?"

"Just fix it, Jessup. Let's get this one in motion." Barrabas hung up the phone.

In New York City, Jessup listened to the dial tone for a moment, then hung up his phone also. He grinned, pleased that he had Barrabas. He reached for the phone again to call Washington. The Committee needed to be alerted. The mission was a go!

As Jessup sat at his desk and waited for the long-distance call to go through, he thought about Colonel Nile Barrabas, very much a one-of-a-kind man, and what it could be that would send him to Paris.

9

Dr. Leona Hatton didn't like medical conventions. They were filled with stuffy old men or young, eager smartass ones with boundless enthusiasm for coming up with magical, medical answers to life's problems. The seminars and conferences could become long and drawn out, often turning into personal arguments between bullheaded opponents who thought they had all the knowledge in the universe. They were usually just stubborn and set in their ways and didn't know squat about the real world.

This convention was no exception, Lee acknowledged as she sat in the audience and listened to a lawyer's self-serving pitch about liability insurance and ways of milking the government for every penny you could get. Don't make house calls, he advised. Let the government insurance people come to you. Always do your paperwork before you do any healing.

Lee sighed and placed her face in her hands and rubbed vigorously. She performed a quick shiatsu massage to get the tightness out of her face muscles. She unobtrusively went through a relaxation exercise; breathe deeply in through the nose, hold to the count of six and exhale through the mouth. She felt the stress of the past three days, the sitting and listening and pretending to be interested in conversations. She needed to go up to her room for a yoga session, some stretching and maybe some isometrics to get the tension out of her body.

The convention was called the UN Conference on Medicine for a Global Community, and was sponsored by the United Nations. The aim was to bring the medical communities from around the world together to talk about better health on a global level. It had its heart in the right place. Lee had thought it was an excellent concept and her experiences could possibly be of some value in the discussions.

She was wrong. It was turning out to be nothing more than another medical convention where doctors and lawyers and other members of the profession would talk about how to make more money and have more time to sail their boats and play golf. It was just structured medicine, everything Lee hated about her chosen profession.

She wasn't enjoying the ongoing lecture, nor was she getting anything constructive out of it. All she had learned in three days was how to keep from getting sued by performing the bare minimum on a patient. Why Try Too Hard and Take a Chance? was the motto.

Then she had made the mistake of bringing William Starfoot II and Liam O'Toole with her to New York. Her two partners were between jobs, as was she, and needed a diversion before the next war popped up. When Lee had made the mistake of announcing that she was going to the city for a week, her two fellow

SOBs eagerly volunteered to go along and make sure she wasn't accosted.

The concern wasn't over Lee's safety; the two mercs knew she could handle herself and would be about as safe as an armored rocket carrier in the city. They thought New York could be a good place to relax between missions.

Lee didn't buy their stories, but gave it some consideration. After some long thought, though in retrospect not enough, she consented and informed them that they could come with her.

Much like the convention, that proved to be a mistake. Billy and Liam hit the city with about the same results as a minor tornado. They settled into the midtown hotel where the convention was held and immediately devoted themselves to R & R... meaning drinking, tearing up bars and chasing women.

Yes, she thought, the two SOBs had made a nuisance of themselves with the nurses, for sure. She shuddered at recalling some of her teammates' antics, then Lee Hatton took another deep breath and closed her eyes. She did some visualization exercises, dreaming about an endless beach, a warm sun and a tropical breeze. She wanted to forget where she was, put the two mercs out of her mind and not think about what they could be doing at this very moment... and just relax, at least for a brief moment. Then maybe she could concentrate on the lecture.

It didn't work. The lawyer was as professionally crude and boring as ever. She needed to go up to her room for some yoga and a shower.

She excused herself and left the conference hall as quietly as possible. She didn't bother with the elevator in the lobby but took the stairs up to her room on the fifteenth floor at a brisk trot. The exercise felt good.

Inside the room, she locked the door and quickly stripped. She began some deep-breathing exercises and some isometrics to get her muscles into a relaxation mode. She was just about to start some serious meditation when there was a knock on the door.

"Damn!" she whispered. Maybe if she kept quiet, whoever it was would go away.

The knock came again. "Leona? Are you all right?"

It was Hulbert, the psychiatrist from Maine. He had been trying to get in her good graces for the past three days. He was just another bore.

Lee sighed and thought, why fight it? She got up and put on a robe.

When she opened the door, Hulbert was standing there, his features arranged to convey a worried expression. "Hello, Dr. Hulbert," said Lee.

"Leona. We were concerned. You left the lecture in such a hurry. We were all wondering if you were suddenly ill."

Just sick of all the nonsense, she thought. Aloud she said, "I'm fine. A bit tired."

She started to close the door. "Thank you for the concern..." But Hulbert was already pushing his way into her room, ignoring the annoyed look that started to cross her face.

"Leona, I'd still like to talk to you about your grief. I seriously believe we can work a session into our schedule over the next four days. There's a recess on Friday, between meetings on the new tax laws. We could get together in my room, and I can probably make a few suggestions to help you forget the loss of your friend."

Hulbert was referring to Geoff Bishop, Lee's lover and fellow adventurer in the SOBs who had died on a mission, not all that long ago. She was still taking the loss very hard.

Lee sighed. "I just don't know, Doctor..."

"Call me Ray. Please."

"Ray... I'm sorry. I don't think a session with you is what I need right now."

"Leona. Trust me. I know what's best in a case like yours."

Then Dr. Ray Hulbert, psychiatrist, acted on a very stupid miscalculation. He put a hand on Lee Hatton's right hip.

There was some movement, possibly judo, and the next thing he knew, he was sitting in the hallway. Stunned, he sat still for a moment, then hearing a discreet cough from behind him, turned and stared up into Billy Two's face.

"Say, buddy? Is the lady getting rough with you?" asked Billy with a wide grin.

"Ugh!" muttered Hulbert, trying to stand up and regain his composure.

Billy shook his head and helped by giving him a hand. "I swear! I have to watch her every moment!"

Hulbert stood up, looked questioningly at Leona, then shook his head in a puzzled manner. "Well, see you," he said before moving down the hall. When the elevator doors slid shut behind him, she turned to the Osage.

"Oh, right! And have you accosted any nurses today, Billy?"

Billy Two shrugged. "I'm afraid there's no time for that now. The colonel just called. We're needed. There's a job."

Thank God, thought Lee. Best to get out of New York before they were all in prison. "Where are we going?"

"Berlin. It sounds like a lost spook in the heat."

Lee spread her hands, palms up. "I'll start packing. Where's O'Toole?"

"The last time I saw him, he was planning to hold a poetry reading in the women's lounge."

Lee closed her eyes and breathed deeply. "Yes, well . . . find him, Billy, and let's get out of here."

Billy smiled and headed down the hall. When he looked back, he saw Lee Hatton leaning against the door. She saluted the Indian and smartly marched through the door. She was going to break out of this numbing boredom and go back to her world of guns, manhunts and soldiers.

10

The three recruiters had the audacity to wear the uniforms of the outfits they had once served in. Two had been with the Legion and one was former British Strategic Air Service. They were all armed to the teeth.

Barrabas entered the room and took a quick scan. There were three of them: one behind a table doing some paperwork, one in a chair reading a skin magazine and one lounging by the window. They wore their uniforms with an air of nonchalance and disrespect. They had handguns and knives on their belts, and a MAC-10 was lying on the floor under the oak table.

Barrabas pulled on the strap of the leather haversack riding comfortably under his left arm. He felt the weight of his Browning Hi-Power in the shoulder rig under his bush jacket. He could stay in front of the table and have the room to move quickly while keeping close enough to the three mercenaries to control the fight . . . if it came to that.

"I heard you guys were recruiting for a job in Scotland," Barrabas said. "I want to sign on."

The one in the chair set the magazine down and gave Barrabas a look of astonishment. "I'll be damned! Christ, you must be crazy!"

The one sitting behind the desk, the Brit, looked up and grinned. He tapped the pen he had been using on the wood, making an annoying staccato drumming. "Nile Barrabas. We thought you'd be dead by now."

Barrabas shrugged. "Sorry I didn't cooperate." He stepped up to the table and reached inside the haversack. The three recruiters reached for their weapons out of pure instinct. "Easy, boys," Barrabas said. He withdrew the face mask and GSX goggles he had confiscated after the battle in Amsterdam. He casually tossed the gear on the table. "I thought I'd return this."

The legionnaire by the window had gone white. "That...is my brother's gear!" He turned back to stare outside for a moment and hide his emotions. The sounds of Paris in midafternoon wafted into the little room and seemed loud in the sudden silence.

They were in a hotel room just off the Place du Tertre. Barrabas had remembered the French Army soldier in Fouguets telling him that Major Bay had men recruiting enlistments into his private army for a security job in Scotland. Talking to a few of Bay's men would be an easy way to find out what Bay was up to and why he wanted Barrabas killed. Barrabas also hoped to get some type of lead to Ilya Valentin, though he knew that to be a real long shot.

Barrabas took a step back away from the table to give himself some elbow room again. He was certain there would be a fight now.

"I killed the man who was wearing this mask. He was part of a hunt-and-assassinate team sent after me.

We fought on the streets in Amsterdam. This man died in battle, like a true soldier."

The merc by the window leaned his weight against the glass. His shoulders sagged. "You son of a bitch," he said weakly.

Barrabas decided to play on the weak link. He addressed the grieving man by the window. "Why was your brother trying to kill me?"

The soldier behind the table intervened. "Why should we know that?"

"Because you men are all members of Major Richard Emerson Bay's private forces," Barrabas replied. "That gear I took from the man trying to kill me is used at Bay's mercenary training and survival school in Ireland. It has the tag of a Bay Team class-seven soldier inside it." Barrabas allowed a contemptuous look to cross his face. "It takes more than a half-baked, seventh-class warrior to handle me."

He got the reaction he wanted. The man by the window turned and rushed him. "You bastard!"

Barrabas was ready for him. He spun about and caught the rushing man with a clean, swift kick to the crotch. The infuriated merc immediately doubled up and dropped onto the worn, dirty rug. He gulped for air, jerked in a spasm of pain and began to vomit.

The one behind the worktable was reaching for the MAC-10. Barrabas whirled again, pulled the Browning and pointed it at the Brit's face. "Don't," Barrabas commanded.

The mercenary sat back up, and the MAC-10 remained on the floor.

"Why did the major send those men to kill me?" Barrabas kept the Browning aimed at the merc's nose. He decided to make things a bit more in his favor and moved the Ingram out from under the table with his left foot and kicked it to the opposite side of the room.

The one at the chair was now standing, just itching to get into it. His hands hovered over his weapons, his left inches from a Tracker survival knife, his right hovering over his holstered Colt.

Barrabas knew he couldn't remain in that rattrap for long without trouble. He would need to act fast, get his answers and get out. He waved the Browning menacingly. "Talk to me."

"You're interfering with a job the major's conducting," explained the SAS man.

"I'm not on a mission."

"Don't bullshit us, Barrabas. You're working on an NSA contract."

So it was Ilya Valentin! Good. At least Barrabas knew that much now. He decided to press his luck and try for more. "How did Bay know I was approached on the Valentin hunt?"

"The major has his sources. We have someone in place, real close to one Gerald Southworth. He is the man that your president has assigned to control the hunt for Valentin."

So "Jerry" Southworth was on top of this one. He was the President's closest advisor in NSA. The big man must want Valentin pretty bad to put the top guns onto the hunt.

Barrabas was getting answers, but the man at the chair was about ready to act. He should get out now, while there was still no bloodshed.

But he pressed one more time, going for the big one. "Where is Valentin now?"

The Brit shook his head and grinned. "Sorry, Barrabas. The game is over."

The man retching on the floor had moved. Barrabas felt the claws grab his slacks, strong hands wrapping around his ankles, moving up and digging into his shins. He had pressed his luck too far and had been caught off guard. He thought he had put the one on the floor out for a while, but the man was so full of vengeance that he had acted, even though he was in the grip of tremendous pain. He had crawled up to Barrabas and now had him in a tight, digging grip.

Barrabas was off balance and about to go down. The merc by the chair was drawing the Colt. As Barrabas started to fall, he turned and shot the legionnaire in the stomach. The mercenary grunted and toppled backward, hitting the chair and flipping over. The Colt remained in its holster. The merc cried out and gargled as the blood filled his mouth.

The SAS man behind the table charged. He kicked up and off his chair, vaulting over the table and catching Barrabas around his torso. The momentum and extra weight completed the job gravity had started, and Barrabas went down.

They squirmed around in silent desperation, each trying to gain the advantage that would spell death for the other. The Browning was knocked out of Barrabas's grip. The other two were still armed and trying to hold the powerful mercenary down while reaching one of their weapons. Barrabas couldn't allow that to happen, or he would be through.

The Brit brought his right hand up and dug into Barrabas's face, going for the eyes. Dig out his eyes, and Barrabas would be useless.

Barrabas twisted his head. He kept the movement going, through his shoulders and back. He turned on the floor and lifted his right leg up, scissoring, using his powerful thigh muscles. He kicked the man at his feet in the jaw. The merc gave off a bloodcurdling scream and spit out blood and mangled tissue. He let go of Barrabas's legs and grabbed his own neck. He was gagging and choking on his blood.

The Brit was trying to bash Barrabas's head on the floor, but the carpet was soft enough to cushion the impact. Barrabas cursed and tried to twist around some more, to no avail. The SAS soldier had him pinned tight.

The British mercenary finally had a grip on his side arm and was beginning to draw. It was a Detonics Combat Master with a full clip. Barrabas had only seconds to prevent the discharge.

His head, which the opponent continued to pound on the floor, ached tremendously. He was bleeding from cuts and gashes accumulated during the fight. He was starting to weaken.

The British merc began to laugh. He put his full weight on Barrabas's head, holding it tight against the rug while he raised the Combat Master .45. He was going to shoot Barrabas in the neck and let him drown in his blood in retribution for the man dying a few feet away. "See you in hell, Barrabas," he said, and pulled the trigger.

The .45 fired and blew a hole in the floor. Barrabas had waited to the last possible moment, when the killer would ease his relentless grip just a bit, letting the colonel twist desperately, roll and topple the other merc. The Brit cursed as he lost his balance. His right hand went to the floor for support, and the left was able to swing the .45 around for another shot. Barrabas cooperated, twisting back to look directly at the muzzle of the gun. The SAS merc grinned, laughed again and then an astonished look crossed his face. He hadn't seen or felt Barrabas grab his survival knife. It plunged into his uniform, going smoothly between the ribs and into the left lung. The man gasped, and after a brief convulsion, his dead body fell away.

Barrabas rolled sideways and stood up, gulping air. He stood for a moment, until his vision was clear, then surveyed the carnage. All three of Bay's recruiters were dead. He had hoped it wouldn't come to this.

Sirens sounded in the distance, their wailing drawing closer and announcing new arrivals. He had to get out or he wouldn't make it to Berlin in time for the rendezvous with his team.

Barrabas picked up his Browning and shouldered it. He grabbed his haversack, gave one last look at the aftermath of battle, stepped over a body and left the hotel room.

BACK AT HIS ROOM in the Royale Hotel, Barrabas called Jessup in New York and told him what he had learned from Bay's men.

"It's bad news, Barrabas," Jessup said. "Richard Bay is one sincerely nasty bastard."

"I've heard a lot about him," Barrabas replied. "He's Australian, formerly with an elite commando unit in the Nam, then a member of the British SAS, where he earned the rank of major. Later, when he was caught torturing two Iranian terrorists, he was busted down to lieutenant and he angrily resigned from the service. He kept his rank of major and started doing mercenary work. He's built his reputation over the years as a soldier without conscience, taking any dirty job that pays well enough."

"Amen to that," Jessup agreed. "Major Bay has a particularly nasty record. The jobs we know about include assisting government death squads in South Africa, escorting drug caravans in Afghanistan and training Libyan terrorists on his farm in Ireland. But Bay is a mercenary, obviously working for someone. We know it's not the Russians—they would use their own forces and never hire a free-lancer like Bay."

"That's the next question," Barrabas said. "Who is Bay working for? We learn that and we'll most likely also learn where Ilya Valentin is being held."

"And you think Isaac might be able to help?"

"Not necessarily. But the man trying to kill Isaac certainly can."

"Yes, agreed."

"Have you contacted your person in West Berlin, Jessup?"

"You are expected tomorrow afternoon. Did you pull together the team?"

"Yes. They are meeting me in Berlin tomorrow. I want to be across the border within twenty-four hours."

Jessup covered the telephone receiver and gave off a shuddering sigh. Barrabas and his SOBs going into East Berlin. The concept made him very nervous. If anyone was able to disrupt diplomatic relations, it was just that group of daredevils.

11

The agent known as Albie felt very uncomfortable. The two men, sitting very close to her on either side, could mean trouble. Jessup had warned her and had sent briefs on ahead, but the reality of dealing with such peculiar people was just now setting in.

They were in the bar at the Steigerberger Hotel, just a short distance from the checkpoint they would be crossing through in a few hours. Albie and the two men were killing some time, waiting for the team's leader to have his mission briefing prepared. She had met Nile Barrabas briefly, and she wasn't impressed. He didn't come across as the levelheaded agent who could get them safely in and out of East Berlin. He looked more like an adventurer with a criminal bent.

His partners were even worse, and on the whole Dr. Hatton seemed to be the best. She was quiet, concerned about details and sincere about her work. She was upstairs with Barrabas, assisting him in the final arrangements before launching the mission.

On her right sat Billy Starfoot II, an American Indian of full-blooded Osage heritage. His file said he was a former U.S. Marine and more than adept at survival and urban guerrilla fighting tactics.

On her left was Liam O'Toole, an Irish-American formerly in the army and, disturbingly, a somewhat notorious IRA veteran. He was a brash man, loud, and apparently much devoted to drink.

It was late afternoon. The mission would begin shortly after dark. The two mercenaries didn't seem to care. The man on her left was putting on a show about getting drunk, and the one on her right was suggesting a romantic interlude before work.

Albie was an attractive girl in her late twenties. She had been a part of the secret community's network of agents for three years. Since that time she had served as a courier for Walker Jessup on seven occasions, delivering information to and from the East. She was tall, built like an athlete, strong and healthy. Her boyfriend had no idea she was a U.S. agent in place, and she never mixed business with pleasure. She had no desire to make an exception now.

She turned her head, and her blond hair twirled around her face as she looked at Billy Two.

"Don't you get concerned before you start on a mission?" she asked curiously. At the two men's mocking gaze she felt compelled to add lamely, "I mean, don't you ever worry..."

Then the lady agent was rescued from the derisive look in those eyes. Lee Hatton entered the bar, looking for them. O'Toole waved and called her over.

Lee approached the table, saw O'Toole's empty glasses and the woman's obvious discomfort. "Looks like I got here just in time. The colonel is ready."

It was all she had to say. The two mercenaries shoved off from the bar and headed for the exit. Albie stood up, breathed a minute sigh of relief and left the bar with Lee.

They took the elevator to the fourth floor where Barrabas had a suite of rooms set up as temporary headquarters. Albie and the three mercenaries entered the room and sat down on the comfortable hotel furniture. The mood suddenly turned very sober and businesslike, much to the German agent's relief.

Albie felt better about Colonel Barrabas, too. He was standing in the center of the room. He had a calm air of authority that would never need to rely on a raised voice, and his people obviously respected him. There was a deep silence as they waited for Barrabas to begin the briefing.

There were no formalities. Barrabas began by describing the objectives of the mission. "In a few hours we will be crossing into East Berlin. Our mission is to find a lost CIA agent who has gone into hiding after an attempt on his life. The man is severely spooked. He may have information we can use for our primary objective, the kidnapped Soviet professor, Ilya Valentin. Furthermore, I would like to bring the agent, known as Isaac, out of the cold.

"There is an assassin on the trail of this agent, as well—a member of the forces of Major Richard Emerson Bay, the criminal mercenary. Major Bay's people snatched our professor. I believe they have him in captivity in Scotland, but I don't know that for sure. I also don't know who is employing Major Bay's company. Therefore, we will talk to his man and return tonight with some answers."

Barrabas stopped talking for a moment and looked around the room. His team was gathered again, waiting to be sent on another mission that didn't guarantee any safe returns. They sat quietly, listening intently to his commands. A flood of memories came back to him in a sudden rush, memories of the past five years. Among the thoughts jostling around in his mind was the one reminding him that he had started with thirteen soldiers in his team. Now there were six, counting himself.

Barrabas took a deep breath, stopping the negative mood. He continued the briefing. "Albie knows where Isaac is holed up. The Agency sent her over under her cover of messenger to locate him after he went to ground. She found him in the suspected place, a small worker's apartment he selected to act as a safehouse. But the Agency has left their man to rot. One of our objectives tonight is to act as the retrieval team and bring Isaac back with us."

Albie spoke up. "I have been working under the cover of messenger for the past three years. I have served the Central Intelligence Agency for most of that time, but I have been available to make runs for other covert groups as well, such as the man known as the Fixer. I have a pass to go in and out of the East, through Checkpoint D, a few blocks from this hotel. It is the route I will be taking you tonight, as well."

Barrabas gave Albie a little nod and took over the floor again. "Albie, Lee and I will concentrate on Isaac. When we arrive at the safehouse, Billy and O'Toole will be street-ready to ferret out Bay's assassin. Finding him is a very important element of this job." Barrabas looked hard at his two men.

O'Toole nodded silently. Billy grinned and said, "Understood, Colonel."

"Good," Barrabas stated. As usual, he left his men no margin for error, and they asked for nothing less. "We leave at twenty hundred, Berlin. Just after dark. Let's all remember that if we're less than professional we jeopardize our mission." He looked steadily at each of them for a moment, then nodded with satisfaction. The team would be ready.

NIGHT WAS STARTING to spread its cloak over Berlin. Lights began to pierce the growing darkness, and the air took on a chill.

The two-and-a-half-ton delivery truck turned onto the narrow lane leading to Checkpoint Delta. The American soldier in his post stepped out of the glass-sided box and waited for the truck to approach.

When the vehicle drew up, the soldier recognized Albie and gave her a smile. "Another late-night delivery?"

"I'm afraid so," she replied with a slight tone of regret.

The soldier looked into the cab, and Albie showed him the pass. He shined his flashlight on it briefly, then gave her a nod. "You get the late shift quite a bit."

She sighed prettily for effect. "So many of my fellow workers call in. They say they are in sick bed . . . which means their boyfriends have a cold."

The soldier laughed. He shone the light inside the cab. The beam rested on the man sitting next to Albie. To the soldier he looked like a typical working-class fellow. Mean, though, and he wouldn't smile. His short white hair completed the effect.

The soldier stepped back from the truck. "Go ahead, Albie." He waved her through, the beam of his light dancing in the new darkness.

That was the easy part. They drove the truck over the narrow bridge between the two guardposts. Albie kept the pace slow, inside the five-kilometer-per-hour limit, and the headlights thrust dual beams ahead like probes that mapped their route in the dark. The lights found the East German sentry standing in the center of the drive like a mythical troll on eternal duty. The AK was slung over one shoulder, but his hand hovered near the trigger guard, ready to pull the weapon and fire at a moment's notice.

Albie took a breath and let it out slowly. She had learned to act calmly in spite of her anxieties over the years, but her palms still became sweaty and slippery on the wheel. "Here comes the rough one, Colonel."

"We do the tough ones best," Barrabas said, his deep voice steady and controlled.

Albie pulled the truck up to the waiting guard, the bumper a mere three inches from the man's knees. The guard walked around the side of the truck and looked through the open window.

"Papers." The demand was hardly more than a grunt.

Albie showed the sentry her pass and spoke to him confidently in German. "We have a heavy delivery to make to a restaurant near Bornholmerstrasse.'' She handed the guard the phony purchase order, invoice and receipts needing to be signed.

A second guard walked up to the opposite side of the truck and looked in at Barrabas. His face came an inch from the closed window and he squinted. Barrabas winked at him.

The first sentry handed the papers back to Albie and gave her another grunt. Then he and his partner walked around the back of the truck and opened the doors.

The interior of the truck was filled with large boxes and heavy crates. One of the guards hit the box closest to him, and it rocked slightly. He motioned to his comrade with a nod, and the other man jumped up into the truck. He withdrew his bayonet from its sheath on his black leather belt and thrust the weapon into the top of the box, hard and deep, cutting into it with a long slash.

He tore the box open and looked inside. It was filled with assorted wrapped kitchen utensils. The guard pulled a ladle out and waved it at the other man. Both of them shrugged, and the utensil was unceremoniously tossed back into the box. The sentry jumped out of the truck and helped his partner close the doors, then they walked around to the cab again. One bent slightly to glare into the truck at Albie and remained silent for a long moment. Then he said ''Go!'' and stepped back from the vehicle. His partner followed suit.

''Not a happy man,'' Barrabas declared.

Albie let out her breath slowly, threw a disbelieving glance at him, then shifted into gear to drive them into the heart of East Berlin.

12

He was about to call downstairs and order his supper from the restaurant on the main floor when he heard the truck pull up to the curb just beneath his window. Isaac thought it was probably just another late delivery. The workers were assigned shifts at all hours of the day and night, keeping the machinery of society running at a smooth and steady pace. But he had to take a look, just in case it was trouble.

Isaac moved cautiously to the window, pulled the old, tattered drape aside and peered out through the filthy glass. He saw a delivery truck. Isaac watched as a man got out and walked to the rear of the truck. He looked big, obviously one of the government drones who existed to lift boxes and load crates. Just another man doing his work. But he did not have the heavy gait of those who do taxing and repetitive manual labor. He moved with assurance, almost grace. He seemed alert, aware of the activity on the street around him. His hair was almost white, and his features were strong.

Isaac continued to watch. Then he gasped and felt the sudden rush of pure joy as a slighter figure emerged from the truck. It was the CIA courier, the woman who brought the messages across from the West. It must be an Agency team that had come for him, he thought with relief. He was being pulled out!

He put a trembling hand to his head and uttered a brief thanks. Backing away from the window, he ran through the possibilities quickly in his mind. Should he go down to meet them or should he stay put in his hole and wait for them?

His real instinct was to run down and drive away in a hurry to safety, but he decided to wait. The situation was too dangerous to go charging out into the street. They would come up and they would know what to do.

It seemed to take forever, and he started to feel a gnawing fear that he had been wrong. Then there was the coded knock on the door, and the woman's voice saying, "Sir. I have your medication."

He gave her the proper response. "Good. I have been waiting with a fever." He unbolted and opened the door.

Barrabas slid into the room. He scanned it quickly, then looked at Isaac. He was one of the most wretched looking individuals Barrabas had ever seen. The agent had obviously gone for days without sleep. His eyes were sunken, and his face had a strained and haunted look. He was thin, and his clothes hung loosely on his body.

Barrabas put a reassuring hand on his shoulder. "We've come for you."

"Yes, thank God! But there is still danger."

"We do have to move quickly. We expect there could be a highly trained killer in the vicinity, and you must do exactly what I tell you if we are to get safely out of here. There is a truck outside . . ."

"I saw it."

"We'll move you downstairs and into the back of the truck. There is another woman in the hallway who is armed. Stay close to her. Move with her. She knows what she is doing. Do you understand?"

"Yes."

"Good. Let's move."

"Can I take a few things?" Isaac asked.

"No."

They moved into the dimly lit hallway. Albie went first, then Isaac. As soon as he stepped into the hall, Lee Hatton stepped to his side. "Hi!" she said, smiling at the smallish man. It was clear he had undergone an ordeal. Lee put a soothing hand on his arm. "Stay with me, okay?"

When he nodded and they established eye contact, she smiled again and headed toward the narrow staircase.

Barrabas brought up the rear. He moved into the hallway and followed close behind Isaac and the two women. He kept the Browning holstered. Lee was the only one who had a weapon drawn; her Beretta Brigadier was in her right hand inside the pocket of her jacket.

They went down the staircase and were nearing the doorway leading to the street when Lee suddenly put a hand on Isaac's chest and halted him. "We wait here a moment," she explained softly.

Barrabas edged along the wall to the heavy door, opened it cautiously and assessed the scene. People were going in and out of the restaurant at the right, and the bakery on the left appeared to be closed for the evening. Barrabas scanned the street with his trained gaze, taking everything in. He then looked across the street at O'Toole, who was hiding in the darkness of an alley. The barely perceptible movement in the shadows alerted Barrabas.

He withdrew silently and swiftly. "Take Isaac back up," he instructed, then reached inside his jacket and pulled the Browning. The weapon barely cleared leather when bullets ricocheted off the barely closed door. The shattering of glass indicated that the restaurant windows had been hit.

Patrons of the eatery screamed. Behind Barrabas, the women and Isaac thundered back up the steps. O'Toole was moving out of the shadows of the alley, his Colt .45 drawn and ready to provide cover. Barrabas pushed the door open and dove into the street.

He rolled close to the delivery truck and was huddling next to it when he heard the second round thud into its door. He stayed low and dashed across the open street, finally entering the apartment building on the opposite side.

O'Toole moved out of the alley and joined Barrabas. "I think it's a Remington 700 with a scope," said the Irish soldier. "He's on the third floor, almost directly across from Isaac's room."

Billy Two appeared. He was at the side of the apartment complex, close to the building, also relying on the shadows for concealment. He called to Barrabas. "Here! There's a service entrance that's clear."

"Let's move!" Barrabas knew he had to act quickly. The streets would soon be swarming with military police. He and O'Toole ran around the side of the building, following Billy. They dashed through the service door and bounded up the stairs.

All three men had their weapons drawn. They took the steps quickly but cautiously. They watched for any movement and made it without incident to the third floor in less than a minute.

They stopped for a brief moment to catch their breath. "We have to catch the sniper before he makes a run. We need to contain him inside his room."

The two SOBs nodded. They slid into the hall and stayed close to the doors on the side of the building that faced the restaurant. They moved swiftly. Barrabas listened at each door, using his senses to find the sniper. He came to apartment 307 and stopped, then raised a cautionary finger.

Just then, a woman emerged from her home and saw the three armed men and began screaming. Barrabas kicked open the door of 307, and the man inside spun about and began firing. But Barrabas had flattened himself against the wall of the hall, and the heavy rounds chipped wood from the door but whizzed by him harmlessly.

"Take him alive!" Barrabas commanded.

The two SOBs moved like a precision machine in action, Billy on one side of the room and O'Toole on the other. They had the assassin disarmed and helpless, the rifle dropped and lying on the floor at his feet.

Barrabas had entered the room and stood just inside the doorway. O'Toole turned the captive around to face his leader.

"So you've come to this," Barrabas said.

It was Jay Carter, the free-lance agent working on contract for some of the seamiest sources in Washington. He definitely was not an agent working for Major Bay.

"Take it easy, Barrabas," Carter said. "We may be working for the same people."

"I doubt it," Barrabas replied.

"There are people in Washington who want Isaac snuffed. I suggest you listen to me for a moment, Barrabas."

"I'll listen, Carter, but on my time. Billy, O'Toole, take him with us."

Both SOBs pushed Carter ahead of them, keeping him covered. Barrabas stepped aside to let the free-lance killer go into the hallway first. There was a burst of staccato sound, and Carter didn't even have enough time to cry out before the barrage of semiautomatic fire tore his body to shreds.

Barrabas moved against the wall and took a chance at peering into the hallway before pulling the door to the studio apartment shut. He saw two men, wearing masks and goggles and armed with army-issue M-16s. He only took a glance, then pulled the door closed, the old wood splintering under the continued fire.

Barrabas turned to his men. "A Bay killer team. But there's only two of them..."

"That's good," O'Toole commented.

"No," Barrabas stated. "That's bad. Bay's killer teams work in threes."

O'Toole understood and frowned. "That means there's another one." He glanced toward the window.

Three things happened almost simultaneously. Barrabas heard the two men move up to the closed doorway in the hall, preparing to storm the room and catch the SOBs in a trap. It was how Bay trained his teams. They were rat-trappers; hit-and-run ambush artists. And there was no question that Barrabas and the two SOBs were in the trap!

Outside, the military police were arriving on the scene. A government jeep was pulling up in front of the restaurant, and four heavily armed soldiers jumped out and rushed inside. It was too late to get away clean, even if they did survive the ambush.

The third thing that happened was the worst. O'Toole was at the window, looking across the hectic street. He wasn't concerned with the two killers in the hall or the police down below. He was looking for the third hit man.

"Isaac and the—"

Before O'Toole could finish the sentence, the apartments over the restaurant where Isaac had been holed up blew into a thunderous ball of fire. The roof also erupted, spraying debris into the crowded street. Shards of glass flew for yards before raining down, and O'Toole thought he heard a woman's screams.

13

The two hit men had waited long enough. They stood pressed against the wall, one on each side of the torn apartment door. The sounds of sirens and people moaning could be heard from the streets below, but the killers concentrated fully on the job at hand.

One gave the other a nod. They moved to the door together and kicked. It flew open and the top hinge broke, leaving it hanging. They entered the apartment smoothly, as they had been trained to do. It was an SAS maneuver, offering a clean field of fire to waste anyone in the room. But the apartment was empty.

The window was open, and the torn curtains billowed from the slight breeze from outside. The sounds of the chaos created by the explosion also wafted in. They caught sight of a flash of material at the window. Their quarry must have climbed onto a ledge outside. The gunmen exchanged glances and headed for the window. It was going to be easier than they had expected.

"Psst!"

The sound had come from behind them. They spun around and saw Barrabas and Billy Two pressed against the wall on either side of the door. They had been caught in their own trap.

The killers brought up their M-16s, but Barrabas and Billy put them down with single shots to the heart. The two mercs were in motion before the bodies even hit the floor. Barrabas holstered his Browning and Billy his Socimi. They stepped over to the dead killers, and Barrabas pulled off one of the face masks and looked at the tag inside. It read, Bay Team-4.

"I'm going up in the world," he stated, then looked toward the window and called, "O'Toole!"

The Irish SOB climbed back inside. He had been the lure. "They were too eager," he said, "and fell for the oldest trick in the book."

Billy was checking the rounds in the banana clip, but he looked up and nodded in agreement. "Bad mistake to make. A guy will always regret it—especially when it gets him killed."

"Let's move," Barrabas said. He turned and dashed from the apartment, his men following at a dead run.

THE STREET WAS a disaster. People were lying on the sidewalk, bleeding from burns and glass cuts. The four policemen were rushing around, trying to bring some order to the scene. The apartment where Isaac had been hiding was burning out of control, and the wails of fire engine sirens could be heard in the distance.

Barrabas and his men stood in the darkness of the alley beside the apartment complex and surveyed the carnage.

"What a mess," O'Toole commented.

"We'll use the commotion to make our getaway," Barrabas said. "First, we'll look for Lee."

"Over there!" Billy said, pointing across the road.

Lee Hatton and Albie were standing in the shadows next to the building. They had a man with them, but it clearly wasn't Isaac.

"They must have captured Bay's killer!" Billy declared with some enthusiasm.

Barrabas saw Lee hand her Beretta to Albie to keep the prisoner covered. Then she moved out from the shadows and onto the street and bent down to help a woman.

Barrabas turned to his men. "Go down to the corner and wait for me. I'll send Lee and Bay's man down while Albie and I get the truck."

The SOBs nodded and swung away. Barrabas gave his M-16 to O'Toole, then headed across the street to where Lee was kneeling beside the sobbing woman.

"Lee..."

She looked up and tried to smile. Her face was dirty from smoke and dust, her clothes ripped in three places. "Colonel... it was one of Major Bay's men. I think he used a Czech RG4 grenade. Albie has him around the corner there..."

"I saw," Barrabas said. He reached down for Lee. "We have to go."

Lee finished applying a makeshift pressure bandage to the victim's wound, then patted her on the shoulder and stood up.

"Lee. I'm sorry. We have to move now. Isaac?" Barrabas asked softly, fearing the answer but needing to know all the elements before executing his plan for escape.

Lee looked at him and shook her head slightly. "He didn't get out."

Barrabas nodded. "Take the prisoner and go to Billy and O'Toole and wait for me at the corner. I'll get Albie and the truck."

Lee nodded. They moved around the corner and joined Albie in the shadows. Lee took her weapon and led the prisoner away. Barrabas quickly told Albie his plan.

It went perfectly and without incident. Barrabas and Albie calmly walked to the delivery van and got in, Albie again behind the wheel. They drove away from the turmoil and around the block. It took them a while because of the arriving fire trucks and rescue vehicles.

They drove up to the corner where the SOBs were waiting. The three mercenaries climbed into the back of the van with their prisoner. When they were in place with the van doors shut, O'Toole pounded on the cab, signalling Albie to go.

Their next task was to get back into West Berlin.

ALBIE WAS BEHIND the wheel again. She drove up to the waiting sentry. The new set of papers were ready and waiting on the seat between herself and Barrabas. The SOBs in the back had changed the tags and crate labels on the boxes to make the shipment's destination correspond with the documents.

The routine was almost exactly the same as when they had passed into the East a few hours earlier, though they were approaching a different checkpoint—the infamous Checkpoint Charlie—so the guards on duty wouldn't notice the same packages returning to the West.

The sentry sauntered over to the truck's cab, looked in at Albie and scowled. He growled, "Papers!"

Albie handed him her dated pass and the delivery forms for the supposed cargo in the rear. The guard checked them over thoroughly, then handed them back to her. He and his partner then walked around the back and opened the doors of the truck to look in at the assorted boxes and crates.

Everything was going fine. Albie was feeling the usual sweat on her palms, the tremor spreading through her nervous system. Barrabas looked at her sideways and gave her a little nod of assurance.

The guards closed the truck doors and locked them. They walked back around to the cab and were about to tell Albie to pass when one of them spotted the bullet hole in the door, put there by Carter's Remington.

"What is this?"

"What?" Albie poked her head out the open window and looked down at the door. Her heart did a complete flip when she saw the bullet hole. "I . . . I don't understand . . ."

"What is this?" the guard said again, pointing. "Where did it come from?" He had been alerted to the disturbance in the city and was instructed to watch for anything peculiar. This was definitely something he should report. He decided to hold them for a thorough inspection.

Albie shook her head so her hair fanned prettily around her face. She pouted winsomely and said, "Oh, I do not know where that came from. We were parked on a street where there was some commotion. There was a lot of shooting, and a firebomb over a restaurant..."

He shook his head and waved them aside. "Get out of the line! We will have to inspect further!"

Albie sighed and climbed out of the truck. Barrabas did the same on the opposite side.

One guard held them at gunpoint while the other went back to open the rear doors once again. He threw the doors open and fired into a large box with his AK-47. The bullets tore rips and holes in the thick cardboard, and a red liquid began oozing through the tears and running down the sides of the crate.

The sentry stopped firing, then he climbed into the back of the van and ripped off the shredded lid of the box and looked inside. He peered in and saw the shattered catsup bottles. Cursing, he jumped back out of the truck, annoyed that his assumption had proved to be incorrect.

Feeling somewhat foolish, he shrugged and was about to close the doors of the truck when he heard the distinct sound of a man groaning. The sentry pushed the doors open wide again and squinted into the darkness of the truck bed. He pointed his high-beam flashlight inside and gave a little start when he saw movement.

Maybe he was going to get some action after all. He called to the other guard. "Karl! Karl! There is something moving in here!"

The other sentry ran around the back to join his partner, but he was careful to still keep Albie and Barrabas covered. He waved the muzzle of his AK at them, making them stand very close together.

The two guards looked into the back of the truck, squinting against the darkness. There was another sound, like that of a man trying to spit something out of his mouth. Then something moved on the floor. One of the bed boards was rising and falling slightly, and they grabbed the end of one to lift it, pushing the boxes away in the process. It quickly became apparent that the truck's cargo bed had a false bottom. O'Toole rose from concealment, lashed out with his heel and broke the jaw of one of the guards.

"Move!" he called to the others.

The guards had found the SOBs' hiding place. Their only alternative was to make a run for it. Barrabas pushed Albie toward the truck as the third guard, who had remained inside the guardhouse, opened up on them with his AK.

As the bullets tore into the driver's side of the truck, Barrabas and Albie crouched on the opposite side for cover. Barrabas reached up and opened the door so he could climb in and chanced a look at the sentry house. The third guard had stopped shooting and was talking desperately on a phone. Soon the police would swarm all over the place.

Barrabas got behind the wheel, keeping low so he wouldn't offer the guard a target. He shifted the truck into first gear and began to ease forward, heading for the closed gate. He would have to break through.

The guard at the back of the truck was trying to hang on. His partner was now on the ground, out cold, his shattered jaw hanging at an odd angle.

The sentry lurched forward with the momentum of the vehicle and leaped into the bed. He rolled with the effort and came to rest against the boxes.

Barrabas hit the gate and crashed through it. The sentry in the guardhouse dashed out and began firing at the fleeing truck. His rounds pierced the driver's side, clanging on impact, and a stray round caught the windshield, shattering it into a thousand pieces. Barrabas cursed and leaned over slightly to protect Albie. He averted his face for a moment, avoiding the flying glass. He kept the truck at a steady crawl to retain control, literally inching his way through the noman's-land between borders, easing toward the West and the waiting American soldiers.

In the back, the guard was trying to stand up, and O'Toole was tossing the bed boards away to climb out of the truck's false bottom. With a mighty Irish curse, he flung the wood aside and crawled into the cargo hold. The sentry was waiting for the redheaded demon. He had lost his rifle during the scuffle, but he was pulling a bayonet out of his belt.

O'Toole yelled and hit the sentry with a full, hard tackle. Both men went down. The guard was able to pull his bayonet free as he fell and swiped at O'Toole's face. The Irish merc blocked the slash, catching the sentry's wrist in his strong left hand and twisting. The man yelled with pain as the forearm turned impossibly and snapped. The bayonet dropped on the floor.

Barrabas drove relentlessly forward. He peered into the rearview mirror and saw jeeps with flashing lights arriving on the scene. Military police armed with AKs were jumping out of the vehicles and attempting to line up the moving target. Barrabas picked up speed as the police opened fire.

The soldiers at the West Berlin side of the border were opening their gate and rooting the fugitives on with a frenzy. They were forbidden to return fire on the Communist police for fear of causing an incident no less than an act of war.

In the rear O'Toole was slowly rising to his feet, pulling the painracked guard up with him. He dragged the hapless man to the open doors and tossed him out.

The cheering soldiers saw a body fly out of the back of the truck and a grinning red-haired man look out. "Here's a present for you!" O'Toole called, and the guard hit the ground with a solid thump.

As the truck drove past the opened gate and into West Berlin, the police in the East stopped shooting. The American soldiers cheered even louder and some made obscene gestures at the policemen on the other side of the border.

A captain of the guards ran up to the side of the truck and reached up to shake Barrabas's hand. "Nice job, friend! You may pass!"

Barrabas gave the soldier a salute. "Special delivery." The captain laughed and backed away from the truck, and Barrabas drove into West Berlin.

WHEN BARRABAS SET UP with his team temporarily in the West German agent's apartment, he called Jessup in New York. He had information that was a lot more definite and specific than what they had had to go on previously. Their prisoner confirmed the SOB leader's suspicions about Major Bay, but what was really significant was that he knew the man who was employing Bay. Superwealthy Alaister Dyce, American industrialist and Communist sympathizer, was the power and motivator who had had Valentin kidnapped. Beyond that, the informer only knew about an Icefort project and that some deal with the Soviets was in the making, a deal code-named Operation Lightstorm. Valentin was being held at Dyce's highland estate in Scotland, but that left things still unconnected. What was Dyce doing and why—that was the big question.

There was a long silence over the intercontinental lines as Jessup pondered the thorough briefing he had just received from Barrabas. The situation wasn't good . . . and that was putting it mildly. A search for a kidnapped scientist had turned into a real circus. Barrabas was opening doors that should be kept locked tight and sealed. Men of influence were not good to tamper with, among other things.

Something big was in the wind. For months the various intelligence agencies of the United States, Western Europe and Eastern Asia had been trying to get a handle on Project Icefort. The rumors were spreading like wildfire. The Russians were poised to do something, and soon—probably within the next year. But exactly what was going to happen, or when, nobody knew.

Jessup was perplexed. He actually didn't know what to do. He had sent Barrabas and his team into the vortex to retrieve a missing scientist, and they had created a greater puzzle. On top of it, they had already blown up half of East Berlin and turned over every stone looking for answers, uncovering deep secrets and the most softly whispered rumors in the process. They had done what the world's most resourceful intelligence agencies had been failing at for months. Barrabas and his SOBs had a handle on what was happening.

Alaister Dyce was involved. Dyce was one of the world's richest men, famed for his romantic conquests and bold deals on the international markets. Years ago, Dyce had become infuriated by America's economic and business policies, and he left the country to set up home base in Scotland. Convinced that America was in decline and headed for ruin, Dyce had made a pact with the Russians.

Dyce became a techno-terrorist. His deals with the Soviets moved in the dimensions of treachery, sabotage and murder. He supplied technologies that included things like transponder devices that could set off bombs from great distances, plastic weapons that could pass through the most advanced security systems and X-ray scanners, tiny compact chemical and plastic explosive devices with the explosive power to completely destroy a 747.

Now Dyce was involved in something called Lightstorm, and it was so vital and important that he had contracted Major Bay and his army to protect it. Jessup could put the elements together in his mind.

Lightstorm was probably the laser weaponry to be installed in the mammoth Icefort military space station. It appeared as if the rumors of doomsday weapons could be true!

Jessup had to make a decision. Common sense told him to pull Barrabas and his team in and turn this one over to the big boys. But intuition told Jessup to let Barrabas proceed to Scotland to continue the retrieval mission. Besides, there were other complications...

First, Bay's men had been using black-market weapons, some from U.S. sources. The M-16s Barrabas confiscated were army issue. They obviously had established contacts in the intelligence and warfare communities.

Second, there was Jay Carter, who was working on a Washington contract. Someone in the capital had hired a free-lance assassin to shove a wrench into the gears. Clearly there were people in Washington who didn't want Ilya Valentin found.

And third, there was evidently someone deep inside the shadow world of Washington. Someone had known about and reported on Barrabas from the moment the mercenary was contacted and given the mission. He had been ambushed in Amsterdam, and the recruiters in Paris had known about his involvement. His cover was completely blown... it was really too dangerous to send him to Scotland.

Jessup knew he should call Barrabas off this one. He should contact Jerry Southworth and turn it all back to NSA, let them send in a team of SEAL or

Special Forces. If Barrabas went charging into Scotland, it could all go up in a powder keg eruption.

At that point in the conversation Jessup took a long, deep breath and said, "So I suppose you're going to Scotland . . ."

"That's right," Barrabas confirmed. "We have the directions and coordinates to Dyce's estate, where Professor Valentin is being held. I'll need your help, Jessup . . . I need you to fix things. I'll need surveillance equipment, special weapons, tools and field gear and the usual resources . . . safehouses available, intel sources at my disposal, transportation."

Jessup sighed again. In his mind he told himself he was totally crazy to go ahead with the mission. Out loud he told Barrabas, "Okay. Where do we start?"

When some preliminary arrangements had been made, Barrabas updated Lee. "We're flying to Scotland. Hayes and Nanos are meeting us at Glasgow Airport in the morning. I'm afraid our job is just beginning. Get O'Toole and Billy moving on this."

They exchanged looks, and in response to Lee's unspoken opinion, Barrabas said, "I know, I know. It doesn't look so promising. But I think we can make something of it. Besides a swan song, I mean," he added with a laugh.

14

Trader Mick was easy to spot. All the other airline representatives at Glasgow Airport were pretty girls dressed immaculately and acting overpolitely to their customers. Mick was wearing an old, weather-worn bush jacket, smoking a cigar, with his feet propped up on the counter and leaning back in a chair reading the latest issue of the *Amazing Spiderman*.

Trader Mick looked at Barrabas, and a grin formed around the foul cigar. "The Fixer told me you were an oddball, Barrabas. Ye and that bunch behind ye look like real trouble."

Barrabas just stood in front of the counter and looked at Mick benignly. The old pirate was a notorious dealer and runner in Scotland. His "shipping" company dealt in every black-market good on the roster: tobacco, Scotch whisky, salt, guns and shadowmen. The Dykstras had had dealings with Trader Mick, and Barrabas remembered Erika mentioning him. He was a scoundrel, a thief and a braggart, but he knew his business and always came through, doing what he was paid to do. Otherwise Jessup wouldn't have hired him.

Mick pulled his feet off the counter and stared back at Barrabas and his people. They looked capable and some of them potentially mean. Mick grinned wider, taking his sweet time about sizing up his new business.

Nile Barrabas was a big man with a permanent tan from the countless hours spent under tropic suns. His dark, weathered skin contrasted with his short, nearly white hair. He had a certain air of authority about him, looked powerfully muscular and had a confident bearing that had to be the result of a superior intelligence. His eyes were cold and burned on Mick with meaning. Obviously the man had seen a lot.

The five characters standing behind Barrabas, his team, were about the most intimidating assortment of people he had ever seen in one gathering. Only the woman, with short black hair, very pretty features and promising curves under her suit, gave him any hope of finding a tiny vulnerability in the group. Still, when Mick looked into her eyes, he saw the fire and ice and knew she had been around the block a few too many times.

Trader Mick was not a man who was given to much analysis and thinking about people and their backgrounds, futures and aspirations. He was himself a wheeler-dealer and essentially divided the people he came across into two types: the ones you could strike a bargain with, and those who could not be persuaded to arrive at a deal by any means, including bribery and coercion. His views were that simple, yet he found himself comparing Barrabas and his team to the people bustling about in the airport, most of them looking as though their time was occupied by the ordinary demands of daily living. The group before him looked nothing like that. They appeared to be tightly self-contained, in command and dangerous. It was clear that their days had not followed the ordinary patterns of existence—making a living, having families and generally following other people's orders. They were independent and of the type Mick liked to call black sheep.

Mick chuckled. The Fixer had told him he was dealing with "business people." Old Mick knew exactly what these characters were—more mercenaries! There was an ambitious gathering of such types up around Inverness these days. Mick and other so-called shipping companies had transported a score of businessmen that way over the past few months.

Yet this bunch seemed different. The others had been young soldiers or lone men from no past, going to no future. They smelled of death and were no better than what they were—hired killers. These people were stronger in character, a close group with a real leader who could influence not only his followers but also the situation at hand. He was a pro with the airs of a seasoned soldier. He wore his rank of colonel with pride, not like a mask of title to hide behind. Mick wondered what they were doing by joining the merry band of scum up north.

Mick pulled the cigar from between his teeth and leaned on the counter. He was still grinning as he spoke to Barrabas. "That's a hell of a shipment ye have comin' to Dalcross. Some pretty heavy artillery."

"Why don't you announce it to everyone in Glasgow," Barrabas suggested sarcastically. His eyes had become stern and were on the verge of being mean.

Mick decided it was in his best interest not to play around with the man anymore. "We'll be leavin' in about an hour. Our hangar is just north of the main airstrip. We'll be using the cargo ships' runway, and I'd really like to take off before dark."

"Count on it," Barrabas said. "We'll be at the hangar in forty-five minutes."

"Good. I can fly you directly to Dalcross Airport. The shipment coming from Kerry should be there by the time we arrive, ready for your inspection."

"That's fine," Barrabas replied. "Forty-five minutes, then."

Mick stuck the cigar back into his mouth and watched Barrabas turn around, speak briefly to his people, then walk off. Yes, they were different, thought Mick. He had the feeling that something bigger than usual was in the making.

He watched as the mercs melted into the crowds of Glasgow's main terminal, then shook his head slightly and began making the preparations for their flight.

Barrabas had given a last backward look at Mick, and as their eyes met, the SOB leader felt he'd be quite careful with the man. But Barrabas was pleased. It felt good to have his whole team together again. He felt right when he was with these soldiers.

Claude Hayes, the black street warrior from Detroit, and Alex Nanos, the Greek SOB, had now joined up with the others.

They made their way through the crowd of Glasgow Airport. Groups separated to allow them to pass by. People stepped aside, trying not to stare, praying they wouldn't be on the same flight with them.

"We have forty-five minutes," Barrabas stated. "Time enough to get something to eat and get to the hangar. I have the airport restaurant in mind." There were nods of agreement, and they headed for the restaurant as Barrabas stopped to let them go in front of him. He checked his watch and started a mental rundown of his plans and ideas on the upcoming job and the proper deployment of his people.

Those decisions sometimes came back to haunt him. After all, he had started it with thirteen . . .

BY THE TIME THEY ARRIVED at the airport in Dalcross, night had become thick and permanent. The SOBs grabbed their personal gear and followed Mick's copilot—a raving drunkard named Cabel who had insisted on singing Irish folk songs to them on the flight—to the storage hangar where their cargo was waiting.

Jessup's source in Kerry had not disappointed Barrabas. A quick inspection of the field gear and weaponry proved that everything Barrabas had ordered had indeed been provided. He knew the gunrunning trade was prevalent in Ireland; the IRA and other terrorist groups fighting the British had excellent sources for weapons and gear.

After a quick but thorough check of his cargo, Barrabas turned to Cabel and gave him an approving nod. "This looks good. We'll keep most of it here. This shed is going to serve as our base for field operations."

"Right ye be, gov. I have a set of keys for ye."

Barrabas took the keys that Cabel offered. "I take it you're going to give us a ride into Inverness?"

"Right ye be again, sir. We have a van up by the office."

"Good. We'll be ready in a few minutes."

Cabel grinned and left them alone. He could take a hint. He went back outside to join Mick, who was still checking over the Mohawk passenger carrier they had flown up from Glasgow.

Ten minutes later Barrabas and his team came out of the supply shack. Nanos locked the door behind them and put the set of keys in his pocket.

Cabel waved them over. "Ready ta go ta town?"

At Barrabas's nod, Cabel chuckled. "Ye're a real conversationalist, Mr. Barrabas. I wish ye would let a man get a word in."

The SOBs piled into Cabel's van, and he drove them the eight miles into Inverness. The streets were unusually dark, the small road-side lamps old-fashioned and shedding dim light. It was approaching midnight, and Inverness was very quiet, the inhabitants at home for the most part, or enjoying a stiff drink in one of the many taverns.

Cabel drove them to the front of the Queensgate Hotel, a modern establishment located in the center of town, where Jessup had booked them rooms.

Barrabas checked in under the name of Sommers and company. They had four rooms on the third and fifth floor, one for Barrabas and one for Lee on the third, and the other SOBs would double up in the rooms on the fifth. The rooms were on separate floors in case of trouble. If there was a surprise attack, it was a better bet the attackers wouldn't be covering both sets of rooms.

They checked in and went on to their respective rooms, ready to inspect their gear.

Barrabas was likewise engaged in his private room and was setting up a command center at the desk when there was a soft knock at the door. Barrabas looked through the peephole and saw Lee Hatton standing in the hallway. He opened the door and waved her in. "Hi, Lee. Are you okay?"

"Just thought you would like some company, Colonel."

"Sure. Come in." Barrabas stepped aside and let Lee enter. He closed the door and locked it, then went to join her where she was standing close to the desk. "Sit down, Lee. Would you like a drink?"

"What do you have?"

"Scotch."

Lee smiled. "I'll have mine on the rocks." She sat down in one of the hotel's plush chairs while Barrabas fixed her drink. When he brought it over to her, she smiled again. "It reminds me of old times...being here, with you."

Barrabas nodded once. He knew Lee was referring to their earlier experiences that had made them such a close-knit group. It was also a reference to Geoff Bishop, the former SOB pilot and Lee's love. Though Barrabas never wasted words, Lee knew that he could share her feelings of loss in an unspoken way. Her reserved nature appreciated that.

Their relationship had always been professional; two soldiers in the world of battle, trusting each other, relying on one another for survival. Yet they had been able to nurture a friendship, a special bond that could only exist between a man and a woman. There was no sex involved—they were both too professional to mess around in that dangerous way. But it was a closeness, a sharing that had been seeded and cultivated since those early days of piss-and-vinegar adventurism.

Lee tasted her drink. "Mmm, good. Thanks, Colonel."

Barrabas sat in the chair across from her. "Is there something bothering you, Lee?"

Still smiling at him, she set down the drink and allowed a little laugh. "You always could read me like a book, Colonel." There was a long moment of silence while Lee was thinking, and Barrabas waited patiently.

It was another reckoning, the pain over Geoff's death, each of them maybe a little less painful than the ones before.

"What happened, Colonel? How did we get... here... to this day... reduced in numbers... and why in this order...?"

"I know what you mean, Lee. I wish I had an answer. Fate can sometimes be a mean player."

She looked at him and knew that Barrabas really did understand. He was possibly the only man who truly knew how she felt about her work, her life and her pain.

But it was dangerous to become morose in the field, to ponder the negative aspects of the job over and over until the stress symptoms could become overpowering and a soldier could make a stupid mistake. And there was always death waiting close at hand.

Lee took a deep breath, closed her eyes and performed a relaxation exercise, quick but effective. She looked at Barrabas and gave him a tight little smile. "What about this one, Colonel. With Alaister Dyce involved, we'll be up against some high technology. The man has a whole research and development center for techno-terrors at his disposal. It's a bit scary."

Barrabas felt a strong and lasting sense of pride in Lee. The woman was obviously in pain, feeling a loss and an uncertainty with her life that must be overpowering. Yet she was all professional.

"High tech is important and useful in a war, Lee," Barrabas said. "But without good people, without professionalism and devotion and virtues, all the most sophisticated technologies in the world won't help you."

"To say nothing of good leadership," Lee added.

"Richard Bay has hired a pirate's crew of losers, castoffs, lunatics and hustlers. He doesn't take the time to train his people properly. Only his Team-Ones are professional soldiers, and they are hard-core criminals and mercs, often killers who mix psycho passions with their work. I have the edge on Bay in this respect. There is no comparison."

Lee gave him another little laugh. She liked it when Barrabas gave this kind of recognition to his team.

"Then I guess Alaister Dyce and Major Bay just don't have much of a chance, do they, Colonel?"

"No," Barrabas concluded. "Not a prayer."

"I JUST HAD WORD. Colonel Nile Barrabas has come to Scotland," Major Richard Bay said, "and I'm quite sure he's not on vacation. This certainly adds a new dimension to our plans."

The flames of the fire inside the luxurious fireplace danced in delight, their light casting weird patterns of reds and oranges on the weathered face of Alaister Dyce. The wealthy expatriate was sitting in the plush chair across from the major, sipping an expensive cognac. He gave Bay a hard look, and a scowl appeared on his serious features. "Do you think they have come for Valentin?"

"Of course. Barrabas just won't give up. He takes a job and he finishes it."

Dyce couldn't understand why Bay was so jovial about the new situation. The call from the bartender at the Queensgate had been a bit unnerving. It did sound as though Nile Barrabas and his team had arrived in Inverness. "Have you met Barrabas?"

"No. But our paths were bound to cross one day. I've heard a lot about the colonel, but it's not the same as meeting him on the battlefield. Rumors have it that Barrabas is insane, that he lost his senses in the Nam. An explosion rattled his head and turned his hair white from the trauma. Since Vietnam he has been working as a mercenary, taking some insider jobs, some of them apparently extremely high risk even for this line of work. He's not in the game for the money, but for the work itself. He's a rare breed, a born warrior. A true soldier. He's living out of his time. His biggest problem is that he has a conscience. He lacks the real killer's instinct. I believe this is the only trait that makes Colonel Barrabas and I differ.''

"Do you think that gives you the edge, Major?" Dyce asked. "I mean the fact that you're a totally ruthless bastard and a heartless killer."

Major Bay chuckled and stood up to walk over to Dyce's well-stocked bar. "That's why you love me, sir," Bay said, pouring another glass of whiskey.

The two men were in the den of Dyce's highland estate. The call from town had come to Bay's clerk, and the major had decided it was important enough information to share with Dyce immediately.

Bay walked across the lush carpet with his fresh drink and sat back down in his chair. "To answer your original question, sir . . . yes. I have the edge over Colonel Nile Barrabas. I guarantee you that he, and his team, will not leave Scotland. As of this night, they are all destined to join the dead."

"Good," said Dyce. He sipped slowly and then gave Major Bay another hard look. "And, Major . . . the sooner, the better!"

Major Bay laughed and tossed back his drink.

15

Gerald Southworth sat back in his chair and rubbed his watering eyes. He desperately needed to get some sleep. How many hours has it been now, he silently wondered. He was at that point where he talked to himself in questions, then became angry and hyper when there were no answers.

He looked around the small but efficient office he haunted in the White House basement. He was spending more and more time there, and consequently, less time with his family, out in the real world.

He had almost forgotten what it was like out there... in that world without covert operations, doomsday weapons, agents in danger and relying on him and decisions to be made at a moment's notice that could mean men would live or die.

He had wanted to be in a position where he could make a difference, get real things accomplished. He was a man of action, not a bureaucrat, not an eternal talker. He had found such a niche in his position at NSA. He had been able to become an active member of the secret club, the shadow community which existed deep under the bureaucracy of Washington's political scene. Scandals, investigations, sudden resignations and indictments left vacancies in the club, and Jerry was ready, willing and able to fill an empty spot when called by executive request. He was now a member of the team which, for twenty-five years, had been active in the dark side of American politics and world affairs. Everything from Cuba to Central America, from the early days of Vietnam to deals with Iran, the shadow clubs were the ones getting into the real action.

Jerry sighed and put his glasses back on to review the report he had just received from the computer printer. It was now almost certain that Alaister Dyce was deeply involved with Icefort. Jerry's intel sources reported the activities around Dyce's R&D facilities in Scotland, and it appeared that they were designing the prototype of the laser system that would be installed in the Soviets' military space station. With Dyce's help, both technical and financial, the Russians could be far ahead of the U.S. in their plans to militarize space.

That was why the President wanted Ilya Valentin back. The defecting scientist could come up with a lot of answers. The new information Jessup had supplied certainly proved that Dyce had ordered the kidnapping of the professor. Major Bay's men had easily penetrated the safehouse in the Ozarks and taken Valentin.

But there was still a good chance that the Russian professor was in Scotland. Dyce was attending a series of meetings and conferences in Moscow in a few days and would be taking the professor back to Russia with him at that time...at least that was the current popular theory. It was up to Jessup's SOF team in place to come up with the answers and, if at all possible, get Ilya Valentin back.

Jerry thought about the situation and had to give a little laugh. What a circus! A team of contracted mercenaries was now planning on snatching the snatched defector from the other team of mercenaries who had made the first snatch! An American expatriate millionaire who was a major supporter of the Communist regime had commanded the snatch of the poor professor to protect his involvement in the ongoing Star Wars operations. Said millionaire was a known techno-terrorist, and the current theory was that he was designing the weapons system to be installed into the Soviets' space station. It was also suspected that this system was not defensive...it could be the President's worst nightmare: a doomsday weapon in space!

If the Soviet Union was to deploy such a system, the world would really know what the term Star Wars meant. Hunter-killer satellites would be launched to take out the Soviet station. Ground defense systems would be desperately designed and constructed in case of an attack by the Russians from space. All ongoing peace proposals and arms treaties would become obsolete, and the cold war would certainly overpower world politics once again. The fear and paranoia would spread, as it did in the fifties with atomic and hydrogen bombs, and later in the late seventies with the nuclear threat. The United States' Strategic Defense Initiative—or SDI program—would no longer be a luxury project, a dream for a wondrous future without the hideous threat of nuclear destruction hanging constantly over the human race, but would instead be a necessary and desperate project essential for survival.

The President needed answers. To meet that urgent demand, Ilya Valentin had to be brought back to Washington. And it was all in the hands of a group of renegade soldiers-for-hire, stalking around the Scottish Highlands, ready to start a little war with a wealthy terror broker and his outlaw mercenary army.

Jerry Southworth rubbed his face again. It was something out of his nightmares... an end-of-the-world comic book plot brought to life!

Then there was the most disturbing news of all. According to Jessup's thorough report, there was a mole in the highest echelons of Washington's political community. Someone had known and reported every move he had made, from the contract with Jessup to the SOF operation in Berlin. Someone here in Washington had hired an assassin to kill the German agent who could supply some of the answers so desperately needed to carry off this mission. Someone, for whatever reason, be it politically oriented or just fed by greed, didn't want Ilya Valentin found and retrieved. That one bothered Jerry. It was the wrench that could bust all the gears.

He had to make a decision. It was important to keep the momentum rolling on the mission in Scotland. Ilya Valentin was the critical key to the entire affair. Jessup and his field operators needed support. Maybe, just maybe, that crazy Barrabas could bring Valentin back . . . and maybe, hope against hope, the answers about Operation Lightstorm would follow.

The decision was reached. Give Jessup the go-ahead and full support needed to carry out the mission in Scotland. He would concentrate on this angle. It would take time to dig out the mole. Time was not a luxury Jerry Southworth had to enjoy. Valentin needed to be retrieved *yesterday*!

Jerry sighed deeply and with some sorrow. There would be no rest for him that evening. He looked at his watch and realized he didn't know whether it was eight in the morning or at night. And what day was this, he wondered, feeling the overpowering pressures and stress. He would have to try calling his secretary to find out. If she answered his call, it indicated that it was morning and she was reporting to work.

But first he would have to make a couple of other calls. He would call Walker Jessup in New York and give him full permission to continue the Scottish mission. Then he would call the President.

As Jerry Southworth reached for his phone, he again wished he had controlled his zealousness.

16

The rolling highland hills looked different at night; they had an ominous and lonely air. They brought to mind stories of hellhounds and mysterious goings-on that ordinary mortals would rather not know. There were always the mists, rolling and drifting and wafting, with the bogs and tall fields appearing ghostly from their effect. The full moon cast its light on the night, reflecting with a strange glow from the fog and casting the shadows of the black men who seemed to have stepped from the darkness.

They moved within the dark parts of the night, staying away from the light like moon slayers searching for a new victim. There were three of them, all black, a part of the darkness. They slithered to the top of a grassy knoll and looked down into the wide valley where Alaister Dyce's estate sprawled.

Lights from the estate grounds fought back the mists and the thick darkness. The grounds were well lit, and men walked security beats around the perimeter. It was considered totally impenetrable by the security force that had designed the system, relying on roving guards, dogs, closed-circuit video cameras and sound alarms so sensitive that they often were set off by mistake.

"I'm going in," Barrabas said. "You set up the watch station and keep in mind we'll use it for a few nights."

"Right, Colonel," Billy Two acknowledged, touching him on the shoulder.

"How long are you going to be out, Colonel?" asked Alex Nanos, the third man in the surveillance team.

"Just long enough to get all the information we'll need to set up the breakout and make a getaway plan. Two or three nights of surveillance should do the trick. I'll see what I can find out down there." Barrabas turned and slithered into the night.

"Good luck," Billy whispered into the empty mist, as Barrabas was swallowed by the darkness.

Barrabas was performing the part of his work that he liked the most, becoming one with the night, alone inside the enemy's stronghold. It made him feel whole, brought his purpose into focus more than any other act. He was always reminded of Vietnam, when he was working in the north country, doing the job that best suited him. He remembered his training on such nights, not just the army's school, but the unconventional experiences, the Eastern men of martial arts, the jungle warriors from forgotten tribes, the professional soldiers who had made survival an art form. He had learned the lessons from specialists and had mastered the ability to stay alive because of his strange and varied training. And he had learned to actually thrive on the practice of these bizarre arts.

Now he moved through the night mists, parting the fog without making a rustle. He silently approached the grounds of the Dyce estate and, like an intruding ghost, made his way inside, while back up on the grassy knoll, Billy and Nanos were busy setting up the surveillance station.

Billy placed an Eagle long-range night-vision scope on a tripod and focused it in on the Dyce estate grounds. Nanos checked their lightweight SS80 night sight, a versatile piece of equipment that could be strapped to a forearm and could spot and recognize an object at four hundred meters in clear starlight.

The Eagle long-range scope which Billy Two was sweeping over the night was also a neat piece of gear. It was completely passive and undetectable and could spot an object in moderate starlight at a distance of five hundred meters.

The knoll where the two SOBs were setting up the station was well within the effective range of both pieces of equipment. Using the gear provided by Jessup, Billy and Nanos could watch every movement that took place within the grounds of Dyce's estate.

The two mercs began the long night-watch, making notes on guard routes, sentry changes at the two gates, dog kennels, spotlight positions, shadow areas and the other myriad essentials needed to make an effective plan for penetration and retrieval.

Peering through his scope, Billy whispered, "See any sign of the colonel?"

"Are you kidding?" Nanos replied. "There's no chance of spotting him when he goes out like that."

Billy laughed quietly. "Yeah. It is kind of spooky, isn't it?"

"It's damned unnerving!" Nanos said.

The two soldiers continued their long night of surveillance. They remained at the makeshift watch station until the morning light began to threaten their dark safety. But by then they had the pattern and routine of the estate's elaborate security system outlined in their notebooks, ready to be studied. One or two more nights of watching would prove whether there could be any deviation or changes in the security routines and patterns. They knew they didn't have a great deal of time: Dyce was heading for Moscow in a few days and would certainly be taking Valentin back with him. But they also couldn't afford to be lax or make any mistakes in their planning.

Nanos was unstrapping his night sight device from his arm. "I wonder what's keeping the colonel?"

"He'll be here in a minute," Billy Two assured, taking down the black-painted tripod. "You can bet on it."

"I hope he didn't get into trouble."

"We would have heard or seen something if he had," Billy said, putting the scope back inside its protective case.

"Well, I sure hope he hurries it up…it's getting light fast."

As if that was his cue, Barrabas materialized next to them. "I'm here."

Nanos gave a start. "Jeez… Colonel! I really wish you wouldn't do that!"

Billy had to stifle a laugh. "Did you get everything you needed?"

Barrabas nodded. "It was a good exercise."

Billy waved his notebook. "We did good, too."

"Fine. Let's close shop and head back to town and you two can get some rest while I begin compiling our data and setting up a plan." Barrabas had a lot of information in his head that he needed to put down on paper while it was still fresh.

Nanos sighed and slung the case with his gear in it over his shoulder. He was dog tired and sorely needed some sleep, but he knew that Barrabas would go back to the hotel room and spend the morning working. Nanos wondered why he didn't need to do things like sleep, like normal human beings.

Barrabas saw his men had their gear packed and were ready to depart. "Let's go."

Morning was approaching quickly, the daylight fighting to take dominance over the darkness. As the new sun crawled up over the Scottish hills, the night men disappeared with the last of the darkness.

IT WAS COMING TOGETHER, like the pieces of a puzzle, forming the perfect design of a plan. The elements were mixed, some good, some easy to work around and others would be a problem. The sophisticated alarm system would be the toughest challenge. The men and guard dogs could be taken out with a certain ease by his team of professional soldiers. The high-tech robots and computers on constant watch would be another story.

Barrabas sat at the desk in his hotel room, putting the plan together, going over and over the data he and his watchers had brought back from the night. The midmorning sunshine was coming through his window now, trying to remind him that he had been awake for nearly thirty hours. It didn't work. Barrabas was concentrating deeply on the job at hand. He was absorbed by the details of the pending mission and could just as well have been inside a sensory deprivation tank, for all the attention he paid to his surroundings.

Lee Hatton stood behind him, sipping from her glass of freshly squeezed orange juice, peering over his shoulder. She was always amazed at the colonel's ability to put all the myriad elements of a plan together and form a feasible mission. She looked down at his work, and she didn't understand all his jottings and scribbles and scrawlings, but she knew the end product would be a workable mission plan. She had seen it before.

"Don't you think you should get some sleep, Colonel?" Lee asked. "You've been working on this for a lot of hours. You could use some rest."

"They're keeping Valentin in a highly secured area in the back of the main house," Barrabas stated, evidently not hearing, or caring about, Lee's concern. "There are bars on the windows and surveillance cameras in place around the room. Not one second of his time is spent without Bay's men monitoring it. The video system is operated from the basement, where Bay has set up a command room for his technicians. He has some pretty impressive tech-ops in his force, mostly hackers and computer cowboys who were caught with their fingers in the data and turned outlaw.''

"My God, Colonel," said Lee, giving her head a shake. "How do you do it? I mean, how do you know all this stuff?"

"I was inside."

"My Lord!"

"I'm going back tonight for a second look around. I'll take Hayes and O'Toole out with me. We'll set up the surveillance station on the opposite side of the property tonight to get our intel from another perspective. I think we'll be able to act after one more night on watch. Bay has obviously set up his security in a military mode, and there shouldn't be too many variables or too much second-guessing to worry about."

"Do you want me to contact Jessup and order any additional equipment, supplies, tools or weapons?" Lee asked.

"I think we're pretty well set," Barrabas said. "I'll know better after tonight's outing."

Barrabas rubbed his eyes. He was starting to feel the chronic fatigue of the soldier in the field. His body was telling him in subtle ways that it was time to rest. He would need all his physical and mental resources for the upcoming job.

Barrabas turned his head and looked back at Lee. "Where are Hayes and O'Toole now?"

"Hayes is in his room, getting some rest and doing some isometrics. O'Toole was immersed in a notebook of some kind with a very intent look on his face.

But he did say he wanted to visit a certain place in town.''

"Okay, Lee...I'm going to get some sleep. Tell Hayes and O'Toole to be ready at twilight. They're on tonight."

"Yes sir, Colonel."

"And Lee?"

"Sir?"

"Try to keep that crazy O'Toole out of trouble this afternoon."

It was Lee's turn to sigh. Barrabas had given her a tall order.

"I'll do my best, Colonel..."

LEE HATTON LEFT Hayes's room and couldn't help but wish that her other fellow SOBs were as courteous and professional as the black Navy veteran. He had indeed been resting, exercising and meditating to prepare himself for the stresses of the pending mission. She passed on Barrabas's order, and he assured her that he would be ready to go out tonight.

That had been the easy one. O'Toole had disappeared, and she would have to find him.

Lee walked to the elevators and pressed the down button. She didn't have to wait long before a car arrived to take her to the hotel lobby.

She walked outside and into the busy Inverness streets. The morning crowds were bustling about their business. The air was cool and crisp, and she could smell the breezes wafting from the sea. Lee had to admit that she loved this part of the world. It seemed fresh, slow paced and at eternal peace. A strange uneasiness touched her thoughts when she suddenly remembered that she had come here to make war.

Inverness was a clean but not overcrowded vacation town. It was surrounded by peaceful villages filled with people living decent lives. The Highlands were sprawling, and Inverness served as an epicenter, its upscale market always busy and fairly crowded. The rolling glens to the north, where Dyce's estate was located, were barren and still quite wild. They were the places where myths had been born, and tales of strange happenings could take form and almost be believable. Lee wondered whether anything would filter down of the Soviet scientist and his capture and eventually become a tale told on cool nights around the fire.

Lee remembered a certain tavern O'Toole had mentioned and knew that he liked to check places like that in case he could get little bits of information. It was in the old, established area, where shops proudly displayed their treasures and keepsakes of the clans.

Lee decided to take a shortcut. She stepped off the main road to make her way through a narrow alley between a restaurant and antique shop. She was walking briskly, keeping up a steady pace, taking in the fresh morning air and getting some exercise in the process. She was feeling good...it was the type of environment she thrived in, rather than New York with its dirt and bad air and spoiled wealth. She was happy, feeling alive, glad to be working, to make a difference in someone's life in the process. She was thinking that life could be good at times when she had to wonder why there was a sudden stinging in her neck, at the back, just above the spine. What Scottish insect caused the discomfort? She reached back and felt the steel-tipped dart and knew she had committed the worst sin—a moment of carelessness!

The drug was already taking effect by the time she dropped to her knees. She reached desperately for the Beretta inside its boot holster and was able to draw it, but her strength was almost totally subdued by the surging drug, and she could barely grasp it in her right hand. She waved the weapon around a bit, then she dropped it in front of her and fell on top of it. She felt like a piece of spaghetti.

Her mind was fighting the blackness but was losing. Her brain was trying to tell her something . . . she had to listen, to make things work . . . she had to get the gun out from beneath her prone body . . .

It was no use. The dart had gone into her flesh too deep. It had been a clean shot, and the drug was in her blood. She tried to think, to tell herself it was just a sleeper . . . she wasn't going to die, was she?

Lee felt stupid. She didn't know what to do. Maybe she should ask the man standing over her.

She looked up at him. She wondered why it was funny that he had on a mask and thick goggles. She would ask him that, too. She opened her mouth, and her lips formed a dull smile, and the last thing she knew before the complete blackness was that the man in the mask was reaching for her.

17

Liam O'Toole downed the glass of whiskey and looked around the barroom for some reaction from the patrons. There were only a few locals gathered inside the tavern so early in the morning. A few were having breakfast. One group was comprised of serious drinkers like himself.

A member of this hard-core group gave O'Toole his response. It wasn't exactly what the red-haired SOB was expecting.

"Sit down, ye bleedin' lowlander and shut ye mouth. We don't wan'a hear any more of yer damned poetry!"

The other patrons at the table heartily agreed with their friend by proclaiming their displeasure rather loudly. "Aye! Sit down!"

"Kiss my Irish butt!" O'Toole suggested, just as loudly. He turned toward the bar and called, "I'll have another drink." Then he turned back to the table of drunk patrons and said, "And then I'll finish my poem!"

The regulars all groaned in unison, tossed up their hands in a helpless manner and stood up to leave. They paraded out of the tavern, heading down the

road to another establishment where they could drink
in peace.

The bartender looked at O'Toole with disgust.
"You're finished here, sir. You're ruinin' my business!"

O'Toole shook his head. He briefly considered
busting the inhospitable bartender in the jaw, then
decided it wasn't worth the trouble. He would just find
another establishment to enjoy his refreshments in.

O'Toole picked up the change on the table, about
seventy-five pence, British, and put the coins in his
jacket pocket. He gave one final look of disgust to the
unfriendly bartender and walked out of the dimly lit
tavern. He had a welcoming committee waiting for
him.

They had made the mistake of thinking O'Toole's
system was similar to that of other humans. They
watched him drink liberally, and figured he would be
at least mildly drunk. They had been wrong.

As soon as O'Toole stepped into the crisp Scottish
air, his head was clear and his mind was functioning
at full throttle. The group of rat-trappers from the bar,
the men sent by Bay to corner and kill O'Toole, were
ready but as soon as they opened fire with their British Sterlings, O'Toole was down on the pavement,
rolling toward cover.

The four men sitting in the parked car by the curb
couldn't believe they hadn't slaughtered the Irish
mercenary. The standard 9 mm NATO cartridges de-
posited their deadly rounds through the empty morning air, tearing the door of the bar into kindling. But
they missed O'Toole.

The seasoned merc was rolling behind a pile of trash, using the metal cans and heaped junk as cover. He drew his Colt and got off a couple of rounds into the car. He heard the men curse and the engine roar as the driver shifted gears and hit the gas. The car sped away with a loud squealing of tires. The four killers in the vehicle hadn't expected the Irish merc to fight back. They expected a clean trap: catch him drunk and in the open. It should have been easy.

It wasn't. One raging killer made the mistake of leaning out the back window to take a last desperate shot at O'Toole. The rounds tore into the pile of trash, sending pieces of junk and garbage flying in all directions. O'Toole suddenly came up onto one knee and got off a clean shot. The killer's left eye exploded. He gave off a soft scream, dropped the Sterling and grabbed for his face. He died before his hands made contact, his lifeless body hanging out the window as the car sped around a corner, narrowly missing a woman crossing the street with a shopping cart.

O'Toole shifted his weight and rested on his haunches, waiting behind the cover to make sure the coast was clear. The car filled with assassins was gone, the sound of its engine lost to the other morning noises of Inverness. O'Toole took a deep breath to clear his head and began to stand up. He didn't holster the .45, and that was the only thing that kept him alive.

The bartender had sent O'Toole out of his tavern on purpose, into the waiting trap. The "patrons" who had stood up and left in disgust had given the signal to act. He was to keep O'Toole inside for a few minutes, then turn him away and send him outside. It hadn't worked, and the bartender was angry. He stepped through the torn door and lifted the double-barreled shotgun, aiming it at O'Toole's head.

"You son of a bitch!" the bartender snarled, and pulled both triggers at the same time.

O'Toole was in Lady Luck's books. If the bartender had fired only one barrel and aimed at his chest, O'Toole might have bought the farm. But as both barrels discharged, the gun recoiled slightly in the bartender's strong grip, going a bit high. O'Toole's reaction was professional. He ducked and could actually feel the deadly shot tear through the air inches above his red hair.

O'Toole's next reaction was almost totally reflexive. He smoothly lifted the Colt and shot the bartender in the heart. The tavern keeper gasped and fell backward through the blasted door, dying before he landed on the tavern floor. The shotgun fell on the sidewalk.

O'Toole was now a bit unnerved. He waited, hunkering behind his makeshift cover and peering around to look for additional attackers. When he finally stood up, his legs were shaking a bit and the sweat was pouring off his brow.

"Damn! The whole town is out for my Irish butt." He spoke to himself, shaking his head a bit, trying to clear his thinking. He had to get back to the hotel and warn his comrades. Their cover was totally blown, and Major Bay was acting, sending teams of killers after them!

O'Toole put the Colt .45 back in the shoulder holster under his jacket. He cautiously stepped out from behind the pile of trash. He thanked God that Inverness had poor trash collection service.

O'Toole became aware of his environment, his mind now clear and thinking of matters other than survival. A woman was crying inside the tavern, leaning over the lifeless body of the fallen bartender. A few brave people were standing on the walk across the road, watching the show. They stared at O'Toole as if he was some freak in a side show. He heard the wails of sirens in the distance, becoming louder as they quickly approached. He had to move fast to get away cleanly.

O'Toole turned and ran through the alley next to the tavern. He came out in the service street behind the shops and darted to his right, taking what promised to be the quickest route away from the tavern that had been a temporary war zone. He emerged on another commercial street and ran to his left, heading back in the direction of the Queensgate Hotel.

O'Toole was less than a block away from the hotel when the hit team struck again. He was again in the open, running at a good clip down the sidewalk. A lively traffic moved along the street, the sidewalks colorful from the summer clothes of morning shoppers.

The Sterling opened fire from a window across the street. O'Toole was ready and dove to the pavement, rolling and reaching for his own weapon. A large storefront window exploded, and the display of clothing was torn into useless shreds. The noise of the new attack was deafening as the Sterling discharged, followed by the crash of glass and the screams of terrified people.

O'Toole had the Colt drawn again and was lying in a prone defense position before he actually realized the situation. Women and children would be caught in a cross fire on the crowded street. The kill team had purposefully chosen that particular street to ambush O'Toole, knowing his defense would have to be limited. But the killers couldn't care less about the hapless people caught in the war zone. The Sterling was eating into brick and pavement, inching toward O'Toole.

A child began screaming in panic, and an old woman was weeping in hysterics. O'Toole's mind whirled desperately as the Sterling rounds approached, getting closer to his body. He tried to roll but came up against a concrete door stoop. If he rolled the other direction, he would be torn apart by the deadly fire.

It was the perfect rat-trap! He couldn't fight back. He couldn't move. The killing rounds of the Sterling were almost on him.

O'Toole was considering making a break, knowing that it would mean being cut down in a hail of bullets. But it would be better than just waiting for death to creep up on him.

BARRABAS KNEW THE SITUATION as soon as he woke. He was one of the unique few who could be awake in an instant, clearheaded and alert. Years in torrid war zones and nights camped inside enemy strongholds and days of hiding while surrounded by ruthless killers had made Barrabas something more than normal. He knew as soon as he opened his eyes that they were in trouble.

He tossed the single sheet off his body and jumped out of the hotel bed. He was wearing fatigue pants and had his Browning under his pillow. He clutched the weapon and took a step toward the door, listening, waiting for the person on the opposite side to make the first move.

"Colonel!"

It was Hayes. Barrabas slid over to the door and opened it slightly so the black mercenary could ease himself into the room. Barrabas shut the door again and looked silently at Hayes, waiting to be briefed.

"There are two, at the end of the hallway, Colonel. They have a Beretta 93-R and an Uzi. They came prepared."

"Where are the others?" Barrabas asked, putting on a flannel shirt.

"Billy and Alex are in their room. O'Toole is presumably still out on the town."

"Lee?"

Hayes let out his breath in a sigh and gave his head a slight shake. "I don't know."

Barrabas finished tucking in the shirt and slipped his feet into shoes. "I sent her out to deliver a message to O'Toole about an hour ago." Barrabas glanced at his watch and thought for a moment. "Maybe she's still with him, or...." he let the words trail off, but Hayes finished them for him.

"She's in danger, Colonel," he said, his tone low and filled with concern. "They have us in a solid trap. There are others, outside."

"Damn! It's Bay's method. Trap and ambush, the same style he developed to an art around the Delta in '69."

Hayes nodded again. "It's dirty but effective."

Hayes was wearing only a pair of shorts, a T-shirt and running shoes. Something had alerted his sixth sense and he had checked out the place, knowing that Colonel Barrabas would need a thorough briefing to set a counterplan. Hayes had had no time to get a weapon and was unarmed.

Barrabas checked his own weapon and hastily picked up some additional clips from his desk drawer. "Let's go."

Hayes followed Barrabas to the open window and outside, onto the narrow ledge. They smoothly eased around the corner of the brick building and onto the fire escape. They ran up the two stories to the level where Billy and Nanos had their room. They moved cautiously along the ledge until they arrived at the window of the SOBs' quarters, and Barrabas broke the lock with a powerful lift and slid into the room.

He looked back at Hayes. He gave his thumb a jerk toward the room next door. "Get your weapon." Then Barrabas was gone, inside the hotel, moving to the beds where Billy and Nanos were already waking.

Hayes inched toward his room and crouched down to open the window. The men below looked up as the black merc was climbing into the room and raised their Uzis to fire.

They were too late; Hayes had gone inside. They waited, grinning, knowing that Hayes would come back outside in a moment and they could pick him off easily. Propped against the wall on the narrow ledge, he would be like an easy target at a shooting gallery.

But Barrabas had seen the enemy and understood the situation. Nanos and Billy had been briefed and were throwing on some clothes. Barrabas jumped over to the wall dividing the room from the one Hayes and O'Toole had been using and pounded hard. "Claude! Check the hallway!"

The warning had come just in time. Hayes was about to climb back out through the window, making himself the perfect target for the two killers below. When he looked out and saw them waiting for him, he silently thanked the colonel and immediately changed his tactics. Hayes turned and ran to the door of his room and cautiously peered into the hallway. It was empty.

"It's clear out here, Colonel," he called at the locked door of Nanos and Billy's room.

"Okay," Barrabas said, quickly opening the door. "Let's move."

The other two SOBs followed at a run, the sleep completely gone from their senses, their minds clear and vision crisp. It wasn't the first time they had been awakened straight into warfare.

They dashed for the main stairs and elevators, but the indicator lights said the car was approaching—most likely filled with Bay's men—and there was the sound of feet pounding up the stairs.

"Back the other way," Barrabas ordered. "To the service stairs."

The four men changed direction and headed down the hallway. They came to the service hall, jutting left off the main corridor. The stairs were at the end of the short hall, and the coast looked clear. There was only an elderly maid preparing her supply cart to make her morning rounds. When she saw the four armed men running at her, she was momentarily stunned. Then she sucked in a deep gulp of air and prepared to let out a scream.

Nanos got to her just in time and swiftly but gently covered her mouth with his hand. "Sorry about that. Can't have you letting off an alarm. We're not going to hurt you."

Barrabas looked at her to let her see the authority in his eyes. "Please go back into your room. You are in a great deal of danger out here."

The maid didn't have to be told twice. She turned and bolted back inside the large supply closet as soon as Nanos released his grip.

Barrabas heard men running down the main hallway behind them. "Move it!" He waved his men to the stairs and waited until they were behind the swinging doors, then followed.

As Barrabas bolted through the doors, he pulled the maid's service cart behind him, setting it in front of the entrance to the stairwell to act as an obstacle to his pursuers.

Barrabas had just ducked through the doors when the two who had been watching his room below came rushing by the service hallway. One turned and gave a fleeting look down the smaller corridor and saw Barrabas. He cursed, stopped dead in his tracks and got off a short burst from his Uzi. The deadly rounds hit the maid's supplies, and rolls of toilet paper and hand towels erupted, filling the air like confetti.

"Here! He is here!" the assassin called to his comrades. As Barrabas started leaping down the steps behind his men, he realized that the gang of killers would be on them in a moment.

"Into the next hallway!" Barrabas directed, then the man with the Uzi came into the stairwell and opened fire. The shots bore into the steps and the railing around Barrabas. He dove through the swinging doors of another service hall, this one on the second floor. His men had made it all the way to the lobby, but now they were separated.

Barrabas stopped only a moment to listen at the doors for the assassins. He heard the lead man calling orders. "Jack, Dell, go after the three in the lobby. Call the team outside! Ben, come with me."

There would be two of them coming after him. That should make it pretty easy.

Barrabas turned and looked for the service closet by the stairs' entrance, reasoning that the layout on each floor was identical.

They were, and he found the closet on his right. He shot the lock apart and shoved the door closed.

Two men rushed out of the stairwell onto the second floor. The leader immediately spotted the blasted service door.

He grinned. "He is trying to pull another old trick!" he whispered to his partner. They moved to either side of the door and kicked it open.

They blasted into the closet, sending soaps, cleaning liquids and paper products flying in exploding chaos. They moved to the front of the room, still blasting everything inside, but there was no sign of Barrabas.

"Hold it!" the leader said, confused.

They stopped firing and stared into the dark closet and saw merely the mess they had made of the place when beside them a door that was flush with the wall slid aside just enough to allow the barrel of a weapon to poke through.

"Surprise!" Barrabas said.

"No!" said one of them. It was the last thing he would say in this lifetime, as Barrabas opened fire with his Browning at point-blank range. They grunted and their lifeless bodies fell back into the hallway.

Barrabas stood up and walked out of the closet. A stunned custodian was standing at the end of the service corridor, looking with wide eyes at the carnage.

Barrabas gave him a slight grin. "Sorry. I'm afraid I left you a mess to clean up." Then he turned and bolted through the swinging doors of the service stairwell.

One floor below, in the crowded lobby, the other three SOBs were trying to look casual as they strolled toward the hotel's back doors. Their guns were concealed, and they were trying to appear like three tourists going out to lunch. But it wasn't working.

The real tourists were staring at them. One woman pulled her young son out of their path, sheltering the boy with her arms. A man quickly cut his business conversation short on the lobby phone, grabbed his briefcase and ran toward the entrance.

"Do you think we look like three happy-go-lucky tourists?" Nanos asked.

"Not a chance!" Hayes replied, looking worried.

"Yeah," Billy added. "And these guys behind us are about to spoil the effect even more!"

More of Bay's men had just emerged from the stairwell and were rushing into the lobby, making no attempt to hide their weapons. They spotted the SOBs, stopped running and took aim with their Uzis.

"Down!" Hayes yelled, diving to his left behind a plush couch.

Billy and Nanos also moved to take cover as the Uzis opened up on full automatic. People started screaming and scattering desperately in all directions. The furniture that the SOBs were using for cover began to erupt, and stuffing and upholstery exploded into the air. The assassins were filling the kill zone with deadly fire, making it impossible for the mercs to come up long enough to fight back.

"Try to get off a shot at them from around the side of the couch, Claude," Billy called over the staccato of the Uzis.

"I can't! They've got me pinned tight!"

The hit men were moving forward cautiously, getting off short bursts to keep the mercs down and helpless. The lobby was now impossibly quiet as the tourists and hotel personnel hunkered down, cowering for their lives. The sounds of soft weeping and sobs of desperation and terror were drowned by the deadly hail.

"Game's over!"

That came from directly behind the assassins. They spun around and saw Barrabas. He had come out of the stairwell and up behind them, and they both instantly knew they were dead men.

Cursing, they tried to aim their weapons at Barrabas but didn't have enough time left in their lives. Barrabas got off two clean shots to the heart with the Browning and felled his men.

The three SOBs stood up from behind their cover. Billy was grinning. "We're sure glad to see you, Colonel."

"You took out the other two, also, sir?" Hayes asked, always the professional soldier.

Barrabas nodded and stepped over to join his men. "We have to find Lee and O'Toole. Hayes, you know where the tavern is that O'Toole was frequenting?"

"I know about where it's at, Colonel. I can take us there."

"Good. Let's move."

They wouldn't be able to return to the hotel for any of their gear or planning materials. They would be on the run, hunted by both Bay's kill teams and the local police.

Barrabas knew his most immediate concern must be to regroup his team and start a plan of escape from Inverness. When they were all back at the airfield in Dalcross, they could continue the original job. But first he had to concentrate on escape and survival.

Bay was good...too damned good, after all. He must have had them under surveillance from the moment they had arrived in Inverness. He acted quickly, getting his kill teams into place and ready for the attack. He was a known master of setting death traps and ambushes. In Vietnam, Bay had been as mean and deadly as the enemy, striking out of nowhere and then running back into the jungles. His teams were vicious and well trained at the hit-and-run tactics that Bay favored. It was obvious that the major had not lost his touch.

Bay was also using another warfare tactic that had been effective since the first battles at the dawn of time—divide and conquer! Barrabas knew he had to get his team back together—it was his top priority.

As he led his men out the back doors of the hotel and into the street, they all saw O'Toole running down the sidewalk as though hounds of hell were at his heels. He was heading toward the hotel when Barrabas saw O'Toole caught in the worst trap possible, one where passersby would be caught in the cross fire if he defended himself. O'Toole dived to the pavement and rolled away from the fire, and then he was up against a concrete door stoop, caught and helpless, and Barrabas knew they wouldn't be able to get to him in time. O'Toole was a dead man.

"O'Toole!" Billy yelled, feeling the desperation and panic as he waited to watch his fellow soldier be killed by the rat-trappers.

"Move!" Barrabas commanded, rushing into the street.

O'Toole was trying to get off a shot at his attackers, but it was useless. The street was too crowded with people.

Barrabas and his men took one step off the curb and were about to head across the street at a dead run when a Datsun van shot around the corner and blocked the deadly fire, giving O'Toole a respite.

It was Cabel behind the wheel of the van, and Barrabas and the three SOBs sprinted toward the saving vehicle, which took the rounds from the Sterlings in the fenders and doors on the passenger side. O'Toole was also up and dashing for the Datsun. Bay's men were leaping out of the windows where they had been lying in ambush and were strafing the van with bursts from the Sterlings. They were so filled with disbelief and anger at O'Toole's escaping their trap that they made a fatal mistake. They didn't see Barrabas and his three soldiers.

The two assassins didn't know what hit them. They were concentrating totally on blasting the van and getting to O'Toole when Barrabas and his men opened up on their left, eliminating the ambush artists. They dropped to the pavement, dead or dying, their Sterlings still discharging harmlessly into the air.

Barrabas and the SOBs from the hotel joined O'Toole at the rear of the waiting van. O'Toole pulled the doors of the vehicle open, and they all jumped inside.

Cabel sat in the driver's seat, looking back over his shoulder and grinning at the mercenaries. "Hi, fellas," the Scottish copilot said. "Looks like I got here just in time."

"I owe you a big one, partner!" O'Toole said, grinning back at the man behind the wheel who had just made it possible for him to have another go at things. "And I mean to pay it."

"Don't ye lose any sleep over it, pal. I'm just doin' what ye're payin' me ta do."

"Cut the chatter and let's get the hell out of here," Barrabas ordered.

Cabel immediately shifted the van into gear and sped away from the scene of the street battle.

"Where to, gov?" the driver asked Barrabas.

"Just drive for now!" He turned to O'Toole. "Did you find out anything at the tavern or did they get at you too early?" Barrabas already knew what the answer would be.

"Yes, that about says it all," O'Toole acknowledged.

"Did you see Lee at all?"

"No, Colonel, I haven't seen Lee."

The other SOBs all sighed collectively. Lee was lost!

"I sent Lee to back you up, Liam. She evidently never made it to the tavern." Barrabas sat silently in thought for a long and pregnant moment. Then, when he looked back up at his team, his eyes told the story of his feelings. "They have Lee. Our hope is that they took her alive, to interrogate and question her about our mission in Scotland. I know it's not much of a consolation..."

If Bay had Lee, it would mean torture, possible drug interrogation and psycho-stimulants. He would be ruthless with any member of the SOBs—lady or not.

But it was still better than the alternative: Lee could be dead.

"We have to find her," Barrabas told his men. They all nodded, remaining silent. Nothing else needed to be said.

They all knew that originally there had been thirteen of them....

18

When they spoke, their voices echoed. The cargo building was almost empty, and the vast space around them was a bit eerie in the twilight. The lighting in the old hangar was dim and poor at best.

They sat at an old wooden table in the middle of the room. One lamp with a dirty forty-watt bulb sat in the center of the table. Their mood was glum and as empty of emotion as the old hangar. They hadn't found Lee.

"I should never have gone out without my weapon." Hayes was being severely critical of himself, doubting his own professionalism for getting caught out in the cold with no gun. He was sitting up close to the wooden table, looking down and feeling very angry. "It was stupid! Why the hell don't I think!"

"Take it easy on yourself, Claude," O'Toole comforted, giving the black merc the best smile he could muster. "Look at the ass I made of myself, getting caught in the tavern by those trappers. I slipped up, no question about that."

Hayes glared at the Irishman. "Two wrongs don't make a right, O'Toole. We're acting like a bunch of amateurs." He accented his statement by pounding a big fist on the top of the table.

O'Toole stopped smiling and also stopped trying to be the nice guy. "Well, screw you, Hayes. We're all in this together..."

Nanos never feared an argument and was about to put in his two cents' worth when he was cut short by a no-nonsense voice.

"Enough!"

The command came from Barrabas. He could feel the tensions building among his men and thought that it was time to take some positive action. It was time to plan and get the mission back on track.

They had searched for Lee for over two hours, despite the heavy saturation in the area by the Inverness police. The town constable had ordered Barrabas and his team found, no excuses for failure accepted! The peaceful place had become a war zone and a scene of unprecedented bloodshed and carnage. Hours after the battle in the hotel, bodies were still popping up. True, they were all mercenaries and hired criminals, but the body count was approaching unusual proportions for a smallish place in peacetime.

Not finding Lee was good news, in a way. At least they hadn't uncovered her body. She was probably still alive, though the captive of Major Bay and his cutthroats. And the SOBs knew in no uncertain terms that they would have to act fast to keep her alive.

Barrabas now gave his men a long and hard look. "There will be no fighting among ourselves. We don't have time to give vent to our rage in an unproductive manner. We need to put our energies into the mission at hand."

Hayes nodded at the colonel. "Sorry, sir, it just went so bad, so fast . . ."

"That happens," Barrabas said. "A mission can go sour at any time. And we should know how often it's happened in the past. But we can't make any more mistakes. We're dealing with a very professional and ruthless army. Major Bay has trained his people to work dirty. And he has obviously trained them well."

There was another silence while Barrabas's words sank in. It was a final time of reckoning, in a do or die situation. There would be no further costly mistakes. The mission would not fail.

"Good," Barrabas said with satisfaction, noting the new gleam of determination in their eyes. The message was understood. "We're going in tonight."

"Tonight?" Nanos repeated. "Do you think we're ready, Colonel?"

"We lost all our notes and intel," Billy Two stated. "Everything was left back at the hotel."

"We have no choice, now," Barrabas said. "If there is any chance of saving Lee, it is through immediate action."

Trader Mick was across the room, brewing a pot of rich coffee. He brought the pot over and began pouring the brew into hefty mugs for the soldiers. "I believe ye fellas are goin' ta be needin' this. Sounds like a long night ahead."

The SOBs accepted the mugs of coffee from the rugged pilot. Trader Mick and his shadowy business really turned out to have made a significant difference on this mission, proving once again that Walker Jessup knew how to select backup organizations.

"I know the layout of Dyce's estate," Barrabas said. "Billy and Nanos conducted a thorough surveillance, and the data should be fresh enough to use in our planning."

Billy gave the colonel his best grin. "I remember practically the length of each step the guards take. It's too bad we didn't get the chance to stake out the place from the rear, but we should know enough to put together a plan."

"Good." Barrabas was glad the mood had changed, that an air of professionalism was again prevalent. He couldn't go into Dyce's fortress-estate tonight with emotions flaring. Mistakes would be suicidal in their crucial state.

"When do we go out, Colonel?" O'Toole asked.

"An hour after dark. We'll use the first hour to adjust our night vision and for observation. We have all the weapons here that we'll need. We have enough fresh info to form a plan. And I think you'll agree that the mission has now also become highly personal.

"Good," Barrabas said, registering the intensity among his soldiers. It was a good feeling. "The first and now primary objective of the mission is to find and free Lee."

"You got it!" O'Toole said with real enthusiasm.

"The second objective is to locate Professor Ilya Valentin and bring him out with us. And the third one has now also become a matter of importance."

"Third objective?" Billy asked.

"Yes." Barrabas paused for effect. It was effective, because he could have heard a pin drop inside the old hangar. "Our third objective is to have a face-to-face meeting with one Major Richard Bay."

"Full votes for that, Colonel!" Nanos stated for all of them.

Even Mick was filled with a rich sense of enthusiasm by this goal. "Darned good idea, ye can bet on it! That bastard has brought a lot of grief to the Highlands! And so has that Alaister Dyce...giving jobs to all that scum!"

Barrabas gave a taut smile that said more than words could. "I've had enough of Major Bay and his rat-trappers. It's time to have a little day of reckoning, and we're just the ones to insist on it!"

It may have sounded like a locker-room pep talk, but as he stared into their eyes, Barrabas knew they would go out and win the second half.

19

The room was completely empty. The walls were all painted an off-white and one fluorescent light burned over her head. Before her vision was completely cleared and her senses sharp, she realized her hands were tied to the chair and she was alone.

Lee Hatton focused her vision. It took some effort. The drug they had used in the dart had been a very powerful and effective sleeping agent, and she also had to fight off a faint nausea. Her mouth felt as though it had been stuffed with cotton wool, and the harsh light hurt her eyes.

Lee looked around. She couldn't move her body, but could turn her head from side to side. There were no windows, and there was no indication at all where she was. She supposed that she was inside Dyce's mansion.

Lee began doing deep-breathing exercises. She inhaled through her nose, held to the count of eight, and exhaled through her mouth. Then she started on mental exercises to clear her thinking. She closed her eyes and did visualization, remembering a tropical beach that stretched forever...the palms swayed in the wind, and it seemed as if she could almost feel the heat of the sun and smell the scent of perfumed blossoms.

"Goodness, but you are a pretty one. Are they all like you?"

Lee opened her eyes and saw Major Richard Bay standing directly in front of her. He had entered the room silently and when he spoke, it had given Lee a little start. She quickly forgot about the beach. She would need all her faculties for what was about to happen.

"Your Colonel Barrabas certainly knows how to pick them." Bay was looming over her, letting his eyes roam freely over her body. "You are rather in good fighting shape," he added mockingly.

Lee looked coolly up at him, but the tendons in her arms pulled tight and vibrant, like steel cords. She was doing isometric contractions, keeping her mind on her body, her muscles ready to endure whatever was going to happen. She continued to stare at Bay, letting undisguised contempt fill her eyes.

Bay grinned wider and stepped up to her. "Let's have a better look at the prize." He cautiously leaned over her and was reaching for the top button of her shirt when the door opened behind him.

A tall stately man entered the room. He had silver hair, and looked to be in his mid-forties. He was impeccably dressed in a gray business suit that accented his hair. He spoke calmly but in a voice that brooked no opposition. "That is enough, Major."

The mercenary officer gave Lee a last grim look, then backed off. "Sir."

The older man closed the door and started to walk into the center of the room. When the door closed behind him, it again disappeared. It was flush with the wall, painted to match, and blended in perfectly when shut. The room was certainly designed like a professional interrogation chamber. She had seen similar rooms in Communist bloc countries.

The man held a sheet of paper in one hand, and before he started reading it, he looked at Lee assessingly. Lee was trying to remember his every feature. If she survived, she wanted to be able to help the colonel find and identify the man.

Dyce looked up from the sheet of paper and chuckled. "Very impressive," he noted. He looked back down at the form and began reading out loud. "Dr. Leona Hatton. Called Lee by her friends. A doctor of medicine. Proved to be invaluable in the field to her fellow soldiers." Dyce looked up again. "I could go on. I shall just summarize by expressing my opinion that you are one fine woman. Could I interest you in leaving the employ of your Colonel Barrabas and joining my little army?"

"Not a chance."

Dyce sighed for a dramatic effect. "I didn't think so. Too bad. Too bad. Well . . . can I at least count on your cooperation while you are here as our guest?"

"Go to hell."

Bay backhanded her, then swung with a full slap, tossing her head left and right with the impacts. Her face instantly became red and flushed, but she didn't gasp or cry out from the suddenness of the blows.

Bay smiled and swung his arm back to hit her again.

"Enough!" Dyce took a few steps closer and gave Lee his most reassuring smile. It was phony and carried a hidden threat. "My dear lady. As you can see, Major Bay has an odd way of treating his guests...and it's certainly no way to treat a lady. Please cooperate. Now, why did you and your fellow mercenaries come to Scotland?"

Lee remained completely silent, and let her gaze wander away in a bored manner.

"I see." Dyce shook his head a bit and began pacing the room. "I think it safe to assume that Colonel Barrabas has been contracted by the United States National Security Agency to retrieve our mutual friend, Professor Valentin. Have you come to Inverness for the extremely rude purpose of finding Valentin and taking him away from me?" Dyce stopped talking and looked at Lee, waiting for an answer.

When it became clear that nothing was forthcoming from Lee, Dyce shook his head again and paced some more, thinking deeply. Then he just shrugged and spoke to Bay. "Leave her for now. I'll decide about her later."

Then he turned around and left the room.

In the rec room adjoining the interrogation chamber, Alaister Dyce poured himself a snifter of brandy and sat in a plush chair. He was mentally accelerating his plans, though he knew that he wasn't about to let a ragtag group of mercenaries stop him.

20

The shot echoed through the night like the crack of sonic speed. Projected at a forty-five degree angle as if trying to hit a star, the 7.62 mm round of the AK-47 assault rifle tore harmlessly into the chilly air.

The guard cursed when he saw he had missed his intended target. "Hell! Missed the damned thing!"

The second guard at the north perimeter fence turned off his regular beat and ran back in response to the shot, cocking his M-16 and getting set for trouble. "What the hell are you shooting at?"

The guard who had taken the shot waved his weapon around in the dark. "Damned bat!"

"A bat?"

"Yeah! I hate the damned things! They swoop ya from out of the dark and can get stuck in your hair."

The other guard slung his weapon over his shoulder again and sighed out loud with his disgust. "That's bullshit! They're just fruit bats and they don't attack people...and they won't get stuck in your hair, fer Chrissake! You have a crewcut!"

The other man was still defending himself. "They carry rabies! Ya can die from a bat bite."

"Right. And they turn into vampires and can suck your blood by tearing your neck out..."

The bat hater chuckled. "Naw! That's just in the movies. All that stuff ain't real."

"Well, I'll tell you what is real, pal! Shootin' yer gun in the night like that is gonna alert the entire guard force. We'll have a panic goin', and when the major finds out it's just you shootin' at a bat, he'll have your ass on a cross in the morning."

There was a moment of silence, a slight rustle and a soft gasp. The second guard had started walking away, going back to his appointed rounds, when he heard the curious noises. He stopped and turned around to look at the other guard. He didn't see the man.

"Hey...Guy? Where'd ya go?"

Now there was dead silence.

"Guy?" The curious guard pulled his USAF Security Police handlight out of his utility belt and shone its strong beam into the dark. He still didn't see the other sentry.

"Guy?"

There was nothing there but the empty night.

The guard walked back to the spot where his partner had been shooting at the bat a moment before. He waved the security flashlight around in an aimless search.

"Hey, Guy? What the hell...?"

He stepped on something lumpish unexpectedly. It gave him a start and he jumped back, almost dropping the flashlight. He swung the beam around and pointed it down to see what he had walked into and found Guy's dead body.

"Jesus!"

He ran the beam over the dead man, bathing his lifeless form with the light. He saw the blood, already running onto the chest, and brought the beam higher to see the torn throat. He couldn't believe what he was looking at. Maybe these Scottish bats were vampires...maybe they did attack out of the dark and tear out human throats.

The guard was momentarily panicked and confused. He stood up and turned around and came face-to-face with a black mass that had just unyieldingly separated from the surrounding darkness.

There was only time for a sharp intake of breath. The man in black covered his mouth with a strong grip, cutting off the guard's intended cries for help. A swift blow to the head guaranteed a very lengthy unconsciousness.

It was done quickly, and the man in black let the body crumple to the ground and moved inside the estate grounds.

THE LONE SENTRY at the south gate thought there were just too damned many shadows around him. The lights over the estate property within the fence were effective in their purpose of lighting the grounds, but they had an adverse effect outside the perimeter. It was dark and spooky out there, and the shadows constantly shifted, changed size and shape and texture. It made for some tough security problems for the guard team.

The gate sentry squinted into the blackness in front of him. He thought he had heard a noise. His ears were still ringing from the sudden shot that had rung out from the north, but he knew that was probably just that idiot up there shooting at trees or rats or something. That guy was a menace, and if the major didn't have such a big project going right now, and didn't need so many men, that idiot would be sent back to whatever rock he crawled up from under.

The guard mumbled to himself something about it being tough to get good help. He blew on his hands to warm them and make them feel more limber. It was getting colder every night. He wished again he had been able to stay in the drug running business in Colombia, but the DEA was on his ass and he needed some work to hold him over until the situation cooled off and he could go back to making the big bucks again. Still, he had to admit, Major Bay paid a fair wage, and despite the weather, the duty was light.

He reached into the pocket of his black Navy pea coat and pulled out a pack of cigarettes. He didn't give a damn if he got around a few rules. The cardinal sin of any soldier on guard duty was to light up a cigarette on his post. It gave away his position to the enemy and took away his precious night vision for a good five or six minutes.

He had a method. He pulled a cigarette out of the pack and stuck it between his pursed lips, then pulled up his collar before himself to minimize the spread of light. His hand was shaking a bit with the increasing cold as he lit the match and put the flame to the tip of the cigarette.

He dragged deeply, lowered the match, looked up and saw the eyes only a few feet away from his face.

"What the—" His hand streaked for his knife, but even as he did, he saw that there was a smile under the eyes. Then he felt the hand at his throat, clutching, holding in a solid grip. He wanted to yell, call out for help, sound a warning. He desperately opened his mouth, and the cigarette dropped to the ground.

The call for help never came. All that came out of the man's mouth was a gasp and then a faint crack.

The man in black took the weight of the falling body and pulled it out into the safety of the shadows. He set it down, looked around for signs of trouble, then slithered away to again become one with the darkness.

CHIEF CONSTABLE GARDINER of Inverness was thoroughly disgusted. It was the same old story when it came to dealing with Alaister Dyce. Back off. Don't push it too hard. Deal with fact-finding, but leave the justice dealing to the city council.

In effect, the self-righteous councilmen were telling him not to do his job. He could investigate Dyce, even put a case together against him, but when it came time for actual action, arrest and possible prosecution, Chief Constable Gardiner was told to turn away. Just let things go...time and time again! It made him want to give up his job and buy a farm.

They were standing in the foyer of Dyce's massive mansion. The crystal chandelier hanging above them from the high ceiling cast dancing lights around them, giving the moment a surrealistic quality. Dyce was there, dressed in a very elegant and subdued manner, calm and cool and sure of himself, as usual. A bodyguard hovered perpetually behind him, big and mean and armed under the cheap sports jacket. Constable Gardiner was wearing his old mackintosh and had his driver at his side. Both policemen were forlorn, yet angry at this situation. They had wondered dozens of times in the recent past how such things could happen in the Highlands and the peaceful town of Inverness. Men like Dyce operated out of places like London or New York or Moscow or Washington, not in the Scottish Highlands.

"I'm sorry I couldn't be of more service, Constable," Dyce said, smiling sardonically. "I have been at my estate the entire day and I assure you that my people have also been here. Could those men who were killed in town be members of a local gang, or possibly agents of the criminal underground? Maybe it's a part of the organized crime wars?"

"Doubtful, sir," Gardiner said. "Very doubtful. In fact, I can prove beyond any shadow of a doubt that those men are members of your...er...security force. I'm just not allowed to prosecute."

Dyce actually laughed, pouring burning salt into the constable's wound. "Yes. I suppose you think you have a problem."

"Sir," Constable Gardiner said, the hatred flashing in his eyes as he glared directly at Dyce. "You are my main problem in life. I will live to see the day justice comes to you. I don't know how or when, since you are protected by a political shield which is currently impenetrable, but at some time you will be caught at your game. I promise you, sir, I will be here to see that day."

Dyce laughed again. "That sounded like a threat, Constable."

"A promise, sir." Chief Constable Gardiner put on his hat and turned to leave. "Good evening."

"Come again, Constable."

"Oh, I'm certain I will." Gardiner and his driver opened the door and walked into the chill of the Scottish night. As they closed the door behind them and headed for their car, they again heard Dyce laughing.

"Damned evil man, Sergeant," Constable Gardiner said, climbing into the passenger side of the vehicle.

"Yes, sir." The driver got in behind the wheel. "It seems there should be something we can do...I mean, we know Dyce was responsible for that violence in the city today."

"Of course we do, Sergeant. But as long as the council and the city fathers want the man to continue spreading his wealth around Inverness, he is untouchable. We have to just walk away."

"Have you had any word from the British Strategic Air Service, sir?"

Gardiner sighed dejectedly, like a man who has come to the end of his wits. It was frustrating for him. "Nothing new, Sergeant. We have all the evidence they need to act, but without jurisdiction and the necessary cooperation from our town authorities, all we can do is continue to watch Dyce and hope he makes a mistake. The British will come, as soon as they legally can—after all, the man is a known terrorist. But right now, the whole process is at a standstill."

The driver just shook his head in silence. He didn't have any reassuring words to tell the chief constable, so he started the car and drove slowly away from the massive house.

Chief Constable Gardiner also sat in silence, thinking about that arrogant and malicious man.

The man had some Highland roots that brought him back to make his home and set up his business here. He already had a ruthless reputation but he had really worked at it once he had become established in Scotland. Dyce was a mega-wealthy technocrat, and he could afford to spread his money around the area with a free hand. With jobs being created and more and more of his money coming into Inverness, the powers that be were more than happy to oblige and turn their heads when Dyce brought in his army of highly paid high-tech mercenaries.

Inevitably, tensions arose between Dyce's people, and there was also friction with respectable locals. More and more, the unreliable elements in his force committed crimes and various outrages. But in their continuous brush with the law, they emerged unscathed. The police forces desperately wanted to act ... and were quickly told to leave Dyce alone. His wealth had bought the council and along with it a net of safety. It was as though his criminal army was handed a license to do as they pleased.

The sergeant turned the police car around in the circular driveway and drove toward the estate's main gate. The night had an eerie quality, dark and full of odd shadows. Constable Gardiner thought it fit the way he perceived the estate, and its owner.

If there was only something he could do... if only someone in the upper ranks would listen to reason and help him put a case together against Dyce. The chief constable sighed and looked out the window and thought he spotted a vague dark shape moving through the shadows, then another. He shook his head, looked away, then looked back again. Nothing. He was tired out by his frustration, and thought longingly of the daily paper and a beer by his cosy fireplace.

21

The easterly winds had begun to pick up across the airfield at Dalcross, hitting the cargo hut with a strong intensity. The building shook and rattled, and it sounded like a war was going on outside.

Trader Mick cleaned his coffee maker with extreme care. It was one of his many idiosyncrasies; he always washed and rinsed the Mr. Coffee after every use. The SOBs had gone through three pots.

Mick had to admit he was impressed by Barrabas and his people. Their planning and preparations for their outing that night had been thorough and professional. The colonel had run his men over the layout of the Dyce estate again and again so every man knew where every guard, dog and alarm system was located. They could have gone into that place blindfolded by the time Barrabas was through with them.

Still, Mick certainly didn't envy that bunch. There were only five of them, going up against a small army of very ruthless killers and criminals. And Major Bay had trained his kill teams very well, also. It was a certain bet that Barrabas and his men would come up against Bay's top killers before the night was over.

Mick poured a cup of vinegar into the coffee maker to clean and flush it out. He began wiping the pot with a dish towel, still reflecting over the men out in the night. He wished he could be of more help, at least offer Barrabas some type of backup for quick escape. But Barrabas had insisted of going in complete, he and his men, a brave and foolish lot! The colonel had thanked Mick for all his help. He promised that Jessup would pay him very well. They had shaken hands and Barrabas's grip had been firm and final. It was obvious to Mick that the man wasn't expecting failure, but Mick couldn't figure out what such confidence was based on—given Bay's overwhelming manpower.

He finished cleaning the coffeepot and put the towel back on its hanger. He was a scoundrel and a pirate, but he was always extraordinarily tidy. Everything had a place, and should be put back in it. He felt very uncomfortable about Barrabas. He couldn't find a neat and clean place to put him in his mind. It couldn't be over and done with...he and his men were up there in the north against impossible odds. Mick couldn't stop thinking about those men. He shook his head and scowled.

At the wooden table in the center of the room, Cabel sat back in the old chair and put his heels on the seat next to his. He took a swallow from the warm bottle of beer he was nursing. He saw the look on Mick's features and knew what the pilot was thinking. "That Barrabas an' his bunch are certainly a crazy lot. They got a lot of guts, though."

"They're the bravest men I ever ran into in this business, I'll tell ye!" Mick stated. "An' get yer feet off my chair, ye slob!"

Cabel immediately pulled his heels off the seat and dropped them to the floor. He set the bottle of beer on the table and looked at Mick. "Do ye think they actually have a chance up there, Mick? I mean, that Dyce has a lot of men hired to keep his property secured. Barrabas an' his fellows will be up against some pretty mean odds."

Mick shook his head again. "I don' know, Cabel. I would like to think Colonel Barrabas knows what he's doin'. I just don' know, and I wish we could have done more ta help..."

"Don't underestimate Nile Barrabas."

The comment had come from the hut's doorway. Trader Mick and Cabel both gave little jumps since they were startled by the intruder. They turned in unison and stared at the doorway, where a lone man stood looking in at them.

They hadn't heard the man approach. They didn't know how long he had been standing there or what he had overheard . . . let alone who he was.

He was an average man with an average build, though a bit lean. It was like looking at a shadow, and even though Mick was peering right at him in the dim light, he couldn't make out much about his features.

"An' who be ye?" Mick asked, squinting and trying to see the man better through the bad lighting. It didn't work. Mick thought that even if the light was bright and clean, he still couldn't see the man. He was obviously a professional spook.

"I'm the one paying for all this," the shadowman replied.

Mick grunted. "Mr. Walker Jessup is paying for my services." As soon as he said it, Mick was sorry. He should never have used Jessup's name. Still, the weird guy at the door did know who Barrabas was...

The spook gave a little smile and a grunt. "And I'm the man who hired Jessup."

"Are ye with the Agency? Are ye the one lookin' for that Soviet professor?"

"Let's just say I'm the boss from now on," the spook said. "You can call me Jerry."

The man at the door stepped inside the hut and was immediately replaced by two others. These men were big, well built and muscular. Even under their jackets and bush trousers, Mick could see the bulge of muscle. They stood straight and looked ever ready, like elite soldiers. Mick knew that the big boys had arrived and that the game was completely changed.

Jerry moved just inside the doorway, being careful to stay within the dimmest light. He paced briefly, then looked back at Mick and Cabel, his eyes dark and his features still completely empty of any expression. "I heard you talking about Barrabas. He evidently is conducting a penetration of the Dyce estate tonight. I take it he's going in for Professor Valentin?"

Mick sighed deeply and thought for a long, silent moment about how much to tell this strange fellow. Then he decided to be straight and honest, because it occurred to him that this spook and his soldiers might be Barrabas's only hope of getting out of there alive.

"That's certainly true, Jerry, but it's now more than that. Ya see, Major Bay has taken one of Barrabas's team, the lady they call Lee. They hit Barrabas in Inverness this afternoon, and your fellow had a bit of a rough time of it. He had to act quicker than he had expected, to save her. Bay is a ruthless son of a bitch and he is capable of anything."

"I know all about Major Bay and his reputation as a bastard," Jerry interrupted. "What about Barrabas?"

"Aye! Indeed he did go in ta bring his lady out along with your Soviet professor. He an' his brave fellows left about an hour ago."

Jerry actually grinned, and it looked to Mick like a smiling ghost. "Good! Good! We couldn't have timed it better!" He pulled back the sleeve of his gray jacket and looked at his watch. "We'll give Barrabas a little more time to make his way inside, then we'll go and give him some support in getting out." He grinned even wider, loving it as the plan came together. "In a few hours, Ilya Valentin will be ours." And, he thought to himself, so will all the secrets.

Mick felt a little better about what was happening. Maybe he could help Barrabas by aiding this strange man and his soldiers. "What service can I provide?"

Jerry looked at the old pirate, still smiling. "Do you know where the Dyce estate is located?"

"Aye, I do. An' Cabel here can take you and yer men up there."

"Good. Do you have proper transportation? There will be seven of us, and your driver."

"Aye. We have a van."

"Great!" Jerry looked at Cabel and said, "Can you be set in fifteen minutes?"

"Aye, gov. I'll be ready and waitin'." Cabel also grinned, feeling good about the chance to assist Barrabas and his team again.

"Good," Jerry said as he turned and walked toward the door. "Fifteen minutes. Sergeant Hudson will give a hand with the preparations."

"Sir!" said the big soldier on the right side of the door.

"Let's do it!" Cabel said, now grinning at Sergeant Hudson. They all walked out of the hut together, leaving Mick suddenly alone.

Mick stood by himself, then sighed out loud, breaking the eerie silence. He shook his head and decided not to think about it any more, but to go about his chores and clear his mind while he waited for them to return. He felt like a Viking's wife.

The vinegar had finished flushing through the coffee maker now, and Mick pulled the pot out to dump the solution into the sink and rinse out the pot again. With the tap water running, he didn't hear the man come back into the cargo hut.

"Mick!"

Trader Mick turned, startled again. "Eh?" He saw Sergeant Hudson standing inside the door, glaring at him. Mick didn't feel good about it, for some reason. He remained silent, waiting for the sergeant to speak.

"The boss sent me back to finish a bit of business with you, Mick."

The bad feeling was becoming worse. Mick frowned. "Boss? You mean Jerry?"

"Not quite," Hudson said. He suddenly reached inside his jacket and withdrew a Tanto survival knife.

Mick tried to bolt, but the big soldier was incredibly fast. He slid over the floor, grabbed Mick by the arm and gave him a powerful spin. Mick tried to fight, to resist the man's pull, but couldn't.

The knife went in clean, between the ribs and deep into Mick's heart. He died instantly, without so much as a gasp. A flow of blood came up and passed through his mouth and nose. There was one little gurgling sound, followed by the familiar death rattle, and Trader Mick's life was done.

Sergeant Hudson pulled the knife out of the body and lowered it to the floor. He wiped the Tanto on Mick's sleeve, then put it back in the sheath inside the lining of his jacket.

The sergeant gave a last fleeting look at the dead pilot, then turned and jogged out of the cargo hut. It was time to go out and find Colonel Barrabas.

22

Major Bay felt like a doctor. He conducted his work with precision inside a white room filled with bright, pure light. He had instructions to try and get more information, then wrap up the business with the female mercenary.

Major Bay had always been proud of his work, but this time he was feeling perturbed. He had failed, to a certain degree. True, his first priority had been to break the woman, make her cry out for him, tear apart her armor and show her who was the stronger of the species. He had accomplished this goal, though he admitted to himself it took more time and effort on his part than usual. Maybe he was losing his touch, he thought for a moment, but decided that was impossible. He enjoyed his work as much as always. This woman was just tough.

But his second goal, to get some answers out of Dr. Hatton, had not been reached. It would have been very convenient to know exactly what Barrabas was up to. It could have proved useful to learn some of the colonel's plans during the interrogation, though it really wasn't necessary. The odds were stacked against Barrabas to such an overwhelming degree that he really wasn't a threat. Still, a few answers from the woman would have given Bay even more of an edge.

Lee hadn't talked. She had called out with her pain and frustration, wept quietly and tried every technique in the book to escape the hideous nature of her reality. But she hadn't talked.

Major Bay slapped her again. "Just tell me the one thing, dear lady, and I'll let you alone for the rest of the night. Did Barrabas come here for Valentin?"

Lee remained silent except for her labored breathing. Her nasal passages were clogged with dried blood. She hung her head—there was no strength left to lift it—and sucked air through her smashed lips. She closed her good eye and rested it.

Major Bay cursed with disgust. In a way, he felt a bit of an admiration for the woman mercenary. He certainly understood now how she got her reputation, but he felt he should have been able to make her talk. He had broken down the best, made them plead to spill their guts. When he was with the SAS, he had interrogated Iranian terrorists, Libyan commandos and IRA killers. They always talked.

But this woman had beaten him.

Bay cursed again, hating Lee for her strength yet respecting her at the same time. He took one last fleeting look at her bruised and bloodied face, snorted and turned away. He would not look at her again. Enough was enough!

Bay walked across the white room and picked up the towel he had placed on the floor by the door. He wiped his hands, then reached for the door handle. Bay opened the door and stepped into the recreation room on the opposite side. Two guards armed with AK-47s were still at their post at the door. Bay waved his right hand in the air, a sign of his boredom, and spoke to the guards. "Take the woman outside and dispose of her." That said, Bay walked across the room, toward the well-stocked bar to get a good, stiff drink. He had earned his pay that night. Now it was time to relax.

The two guards marched into the interrogation room and walked up to Lee's sagging body. She was forcing herself to rest, to not think about what was happening. She was reaching deep inside herself, searching for reserves, some inner strength. She found none. Bay had broken her completely. Everything was gone. She could try to fight, and she would, but the two strong guards had the total edge.

The guards cut the ropes on Lee's wrists and ankles, then one of them reached for her and yanked her to her feet. Then both of them got a hold of her and dragged her outside, and she was roughly jostled in the process.

They pulled her around the back of the house and let her drop onto the dirt. She landed on her back and her head made a solid thump when it hit the ground. They tossed their AKs down and stood looking down at Lee Hatton, savoring their sense of power over her. She opened her one good eye and looked up. Then she did something rather strange. She smiled.

"Welcome to hell, fellas."

They looked at her in some confusion, but the moment passed.

"You have it backward," one of them said.

"Yeah. You're the one who's having the nightmare."

"Wrong," Lee corrected. She closed her good eye and waited.

"This bitch is crazy," said one of the guards, "but should be good fun," he added, and winked.

Something moved. A shadow changed. The man who had called Lee crazy squinted against the bright security light that was almost directly overhead. The grounds around them were a bit darker than most of the areas of the estate. There seemed to be more shadows than usual.

"Did you see something?" he asked his partner.

"Probably just one of the dogs loose again."

"I don't hear any barking. Do you think something's wrong?"

"Naw. It's just a quiet night. Relax and let's get on with it."

The worried guard was just reaching for his side arm when a shadow seemed to move again. Then another. This time both of them saw it.

"What the hell was that?"

"Did you see . . . ?"

"Hell!" said the other, and they looked around for their AKs. They were gone.

"Oh-oh . . ."

The lead shadow materialized into a man, as did the two behind the guards, reaching for them, spoiling their fun.

"Mother of God!"

Then there were only sudden lunges and a tangle of bodies, followed by stillness. The guards were done for.

"Hide the bodies over there," commanded Barrabas, the lead shadow, and pointed at a clump of bushes next to the mansion.

Hayes and O'Toole, the SOBs who had come up behind the guards, took the dead men and dragged them over to the shrubs. They set the bodies in the flower bed.

"Lee..." Barrabas had knelt down by her and gently touched her bruised cheek. Lee opened her good eye again and gave him her best smile. It wasn't much.

"Hello, Colonel. I knew you wouldn't let me down."

"Never, Lee. Never."

She rested, and Barrabas stood back up. "Billy! Take her out of here. Get her off the grounds, to safety, then give her some medical attention."

"Yes, sir!"

Looking serious and concerned, Billy Two reached down and gently took Lee Hatton into his powerful arms and carried her into the shadows. He slid away and was gone in a second.

Barrabas looked at his three remaining men. He needed to instill confidence in them to continue the mission.

"We're going inside to get Valentin. We're going to get him out. Surprise will be our advantage."

ALAISTER DYCE and Major Bay were sitting in front of the fireplace in the study, enjoying a glass of whiskey. Dyce took a sip and gave Bay a disapproving look.

"So, you couldn't make the woman talk," he stated. "I must admit I'm surprised, Major."

Bay waved his hand, dismissing any concerns that Dyce might have. "It doesn't matter, sir. She's gone by now."

"Still, Major, you're losing your touch. Getting soft?"

Bay remained silent and just smiled slightly at the other man.

"Now, won't Colonel Barrabas be angry?" Dyce asked, looking amused.

"I certainly hope so," Bay replied.

That's when the yelling started.

The first cry came from almost directly outside the window of Dyce's study. It was a nerve-wrenching shout, the call of a man about to die. Both Alaister Dyce and Major Bay jerked forward, and a bit of the major's whiskey spilled on his trousers.

"What in the name of God was that?" asked Dyce, and his question was punctuated by another yell from outside.

Bay virtually leaped out of his plush chair and jumped to the window. He cautiously pressed his body against the wall and pulled a curtain aside to look outside.

Dyce followed, coming out of his seat and walking toward the window. "What is it, Bay? What's going on out there?"

Bay waved a cautioning hand at Dyce. "Stay away from the window, sir. Don't make yourself a target."

Dyce flattened himself against the wall, next to Major Bay. "Bay! What the hell is going on out there? Can you see anything?"

"There's too much glare on the window," Bay stated. "Turn out the lights . . . sir."

Alaister Dyce snorted with displeasure at being told what to do, but did as the major suggested. He left his place by the window, jogged across the den and turned off the lights. The room plunged into semidarkness, lit with an eerie orange glow from the fireplace. Dyce rushed back to press against the wall next to Major Bay.

A man shouted, and the staccato of automatic weapons' fire followed, tearing apart the quiet of the night. More weapons discharged, and men began to shout to each other.

"Here! Over here! Jesus!"

"Can you see them? Do you see anything?"

"Oh God! Oh God! Look at Weston!"

"How can you tell that's Weston? He's got no fuckin' head!"

Dyce grabbed Major Bay by the sleeve. "Bay! What the hell is going on out there? For Christ's sake, man . . ."

There was a scream, this time closer to the house.

Bay turned around and looked at Dyce, and the expatriate millionaire gasped softly and backed off a step when he saw the expression on the major's face.

Major Bay had a crazed look on his face. He spoke softly, as if he were savoring his own words. "It's Barrabas."

"Jesus!" There was a quaver in Dyce's voice, and the hand that still clutched the major's arm shook a little.

"He's come for us with a vengeance! We killed one of his people, and he has a vendetta to settle. He's out there now, Dyce...in the night...getting our men."

Dyce panicked. He clutched tighter at the major's sleeve. He literally shook in his fear. "Dammit, Major! Why aren't your people doing something? What am I paying you for?"

Bay just continued to grin. "That's Barrabas out there, sir. He hasn't been stopped yet! He escaped Amsterdam, Paris, Berlin and our traps and ambushes in town this afternoon. He's come this far!"

Dyce shook his fist furiously. "Damn it, Bay! Damn it all! I'm paying you good money for security—"

"You haven't been listening...sir! That's Barrabas out there! Remember what I said about him? He's insane! He's come with a vengeance. The men he has with him are just as bad. You don't pay me enough—you couldn't pay me enough—to go up against him!"

Dyce looked shocked. "What? What the hell do you mean by that, Major?"

Bay grinned wider. "It means I'll take on that bastard just for the pleasure of it!"

The door of the study suddenly burst open, and the captain of the night-shift guard detail rushed into the room. "Major, sir, we are under attack."

"I can hear it, Captain. It sounds like you're getting your asses kicked."

"Sir...there must be fifty of them...they're all around us out there...we can't see them. They're taking us one by one."

Bay was perplexed. "There's not fifty of them, Captain. There's probably only a handful."

"Sir? What are your orders?"

Bay smiled at the captain. "I have a Team-One in the bunkhouse..."

"Yes, sir. They are assembled and waiting for your orders."

"Good. I'll join them and direct this action myself." Bay was heading for the door in a hurry when the guard captain spoke up again.

"Sir? There's something else I should mention..."

Bay stopped in his tracks, perplexed again. "Well, what the hell is it, Captain?"

"Professor Valentin is missing."

"What—"

The last remark came from Dyce. His eyes were wide and his fists were balled up at his sides.

"Yes...sir...Mister Dyce...he's not in his cell. The room is empty. He has apparently just disappeared."

"He didn't disappear, Captain!" said Bay, and there was a more serious tone in his voice now. "Barrabas has him."

Alaister Dyce exploded. He began to shake in fury, pointing an accusing finger at Bay. "I hold you responsible for this, Major! You and your untrained men! I order you to get Valentin back...at once! Do you hear me? And kill Barrabas! I order you to kill Barrabas!''

Major Bay gave the anguished millionaire a quick but penetrating glare and then rushed from the study, on his way to join his number-one hit team.

BILLY STARFOOT II KNELT over Lee Hatton's body and used a sliver of moonlight to work by. He had set her on a soft patch of grass, away from the Dyce estate grounds and ongoing war zone. He hastily cleaned her wounds while he listened to the sounds of the battle in the distance. Time had to be taken out to make certain Lee would be all right, no matter how much he wanted to be throwing himself into the face-off.

There was a rustling from the brush behind them. Billy spun about, and his Socimi filled his hand as if by magic. "Starfoot," came the whisper, then O'Toole stepped into the clearing. Stumbling behind him was Professor Ilya Valentin.

"Wow! Easy, Billy!" The Irish merc flashed a friendly grin at his partner.

Billy Two holstered the Socimi. He gave O'Toole his disapproving look. "It's about time you got here."

Lee Hatton tried to sit up, protesting that she was all right. She pushed with her arms and rested her weight on her elbows. "And this must be Professor Valentin."

The hapless professor looked stunned. Too much had happened too quickly. He was in his cell-like room, reading a scientific journal, preparing to get some sleep, when all hell broke loose around him! Men began screaming, guns went off, and the next thing he knew, a man in black with his face covered with charcoal kicked open the door and grabbed him. The commando literally dragged him out of the mansion, across the estate grounds and into the woods.

Now there were two more night soldiers, and one was a woman. She looked wounded, her face bruised and bloodied. He felt instant concern for her. She must have been hurt while rescuing him.

"Yes," said the confused professor. "I am Ilya Valentin. Who are you people?"

Billy grinned up at him, his teeth flashing in contrast with his painted face. "We're the travel committee. We've decided you need a nice, long trip to Washington."

O'Toole knelt next to Billy and directed a concerned look at Lee. She seemed to be mending. He set his Heckler & Koch SMG in the grass next to him. The MP-5 series submachine gun was the weapon chosen by Barrabas for this mission. It was the model used by West Germans, and Barrabas had got the idea to use it when he called Jessup from Berlin. The new version they were using was a modified and silenced SD3 with retractable paratrooper's buttstock.

Lee shifted her weight so she could turn and look up at Valentin. The professor looked very confused and terrified. She decided to try to put him at ease and gave him the best smile she had to offer. It worked, and the professor felt somewhat reassured. "Why don't you just sit down here and rest with us for the moment, Professor," Lee said. "We still have some friends back there at the estate, and we need to wait for a signal from them before we can leave."

The sounds of the battle back at the estate were as ferocious and intense as ever, with the chatter of submachine guns eating away at the night. Professor Valentin listened to them and he thought it sad that this carnage had to happen in order to rescue him.

"Listen!" The remark came from Billy. He suddenly turned very serious. He looked around, his trained senses working at full throttle.

O'Toole heard it now, as well. Men were approaching, moving through the brush. They were coming from all the wrong directions—it wasn't their fellow SOBs!

"Damn!" O'Toole said. "Did they have a patrol out?"

"I don't think so," Billy replied. "There was no reason—"

The sounds of people drawing closer became louder, more distinct. It meant trouble.

"Ready!" said Billy, reaching for his SMG, and O'Toole also picked up his weapon and got ready for a fight.

Ilya Valentin looked terrified again. Lee took the Colt from O'Toole and held it at the ready in her right hand. She gave the professor a sympathetic look. "Keep cool. Just keep your head down and stay close to me." He nodded in acknowledgement and moved closer to her.

The two SOBs moved to either side of the small clearing, their weapons ready. They all crouched in silence, listening to the footsteps of the approaching group and waiting for the firefight to start.

MAJOR RICHARD BAY led his Team-One out of the bunkhouse. His number-one team looked like a very assorted group gathered from some unlikely places. They were the product of a hundred wars, the results of dirty combat and acts of raw terror performed in the worst fires of battle. They were the best, or worst, depending on what the perspective was, in the arts of mean warfare and straightforward murder. Seven men, a highly trained paramilitary team armed with the most sophisticated weaponry.

Major Richard Bay jerked his head in the direction of the front of Dyce's huge mansion. "Barrabas and his people are inside. We will storm the house."

The members of the Team-One kill squad began to move, getting into positions to attack the mansion when their major gave the order.

Bay turned around and looked at the house and smiled as his men started to get into position for attack.

One of them stood at his side, ready and waiting for the command to act. Bay looked at the hired soldier, still smiling wide, and said, "It all boils down to this moment. Are you ready to really see how good we are?"

"Yes, sir!"

Bay turned back toward the house. "Good. Let's do it!" He was all set to give the command to storm the mansion when the rules of the game suddenly changed drastically. The front door opened, and Claude Hayes tossed two American Mk3A2 grenades with five-second delay fuses into the yard.

"Cover!" Bay only had time to shout the one command when the grenades blew, one on either side of him. Security lights erupted and exploded, plunging the yard into a semidarkness. Earth and grass were thrown into the night air and the soldiers who were surrounding the house ducked and cowered as a rain of dirt and debris cascaded down on them.

"Sir—" the man next to Bay gasped. He had been the first to look up. Beyond that, all he could do was to point at the front door of the mansion.

Bay looked up from his prone position on the ground. He squinted, trying to get his night vision into focus and see through the smoke.

Shapes were moving at the front of the house. Fires burned around them where the grenades had gone off. The security lights were all gone, except for one lone mercury lamp that still burned at the rear of the estate.

The shapes began to take form, becoming four bodies walking slowly out the front doorway, through the thick smoke and into the firelight.

Bay cursed and stood up slowly, staring at the scene that was unfolding before him. The man by his side also stood up and stared at the house.

The first form that took complete shape was that of Alaister Dyce. Barrabas was directly behind him, holding his Heckler & Koch SMG muzzle at the millionaire's temple. Two of the SOBs materialized next to Barrabas, Hayes on the colonel's left and Alex Nanos on the right.

Weapons were lifted and aimed; bolts were drawn and snapped. Three dozen men waited for Major Bay to give the command to fire.

It was Barrabas who spoke. "Another move from anyone, and I'll spray his brains all over the estate."

Dyce spoke next. "Bay! Tell your men to back off...now!"

Bay waited a second for effect, enjoying the way Dyce was squirming in total panic. He knew his men wouldn't fire. Hell, if they made a mistake, there wouldn't be anyone to sign their paychecks.

"Hold your fire." Bay gave the command just loud enough for all his soldiers to hear. He glanced around and saw them obeying his command. He looked back at Barrabas and smiled. "Colonel Nile Barrabas. We meet at last."

"Bay."

"I've heard a lot about you," Bay said. "And you certainly have lived up to your reputation this long night."

"And there are no words for you, scum."

"Ha!" Bay gave his head an excited little shake. "So, the shooting has stopped, and we've now begun the name-calling. What happens next, Barrabas?"

Barrabas shrugged. "It looks like we have a standoff."

LIAM O'TOOLE MOVED a step forward, peering into the darkness.

"Do you see them yet?" Billy Two asked in a whisper.

"Yeah. They're heading for us, from the highway, using the same trail we used."

"How many?" Billy asked.

"Eight. Get ready. They're about on us."

Billy crouched lower in the dark. Professor Valentin pressed closer against Lee. She gave him a reassuring pat on the arm and looked at the trail, waiting.

O'Toole lifted his weapon, ready to open up.

"Hey!" called a familiar voice suddenly. "Now ye fellas have a strange way of greetin' a friend!"

"Cabel!" O'Toole was taken by surprise and lowered the SMG. "What the hell are you doing out here?"

"I brought these fellows to help you. They came all the way from America."

Gerald Southworth of the National Security Agency and his team of Special Forces aides walked into the clearing. "Gentlemen."

The SOBs looked a bit stunned. They weren't quite sure what was going on, but figured the big man had come to retrieve the prize in person.

Southworth looked at the professor and smiled with delight. "This must be Professor Ilya Valentin."

Valentin was sitting up now, next to Lee. He nodded slightly at the gray-haired man.

"I am so happy to meet you," Southworth stated. He looked around at the mercenaries and continued to smile with true feeling. "You people have done a fabulous job! Just fabulous! Where is Colonel Barrabas?"

"He's still down at the estate with the rest of our team," Billy said.

"Well, my men and I will be happy to assist in getting your colonel and team members out."

"That won't be necessary, sir," Billy said.

"Oh, I insist! We'll be delighted to help..."

"Colonel Barrabas isn't coming out, sir."

"What do you mean? The mission is accomplished...and a total success. We have Professor Valentin here."

"The colonel isn't finished."

Southworth was now confused. "Not finished? What do you mean?"

Billy Two grinned. "Colonel Barrabas wants the Icefort project and to get a handle on something called Operation Lightstorm."

23

Chief Constable Gardiner of Inverness didn't know whether he should be mad as hell or just confused. McNetty had never called him so early in the morning before. McNetty was usually a jellyfish when it came to dealing with the chief constable. But this morning, the night shift sergeant had been very insistent.

It was barely daybreak. Gardiner made his way down the street, heading toward the police station in the middle of town, rubbing his eyes and fighting back the sleepiness.

The city was beginning to stir and awaken. Shop owners were preparing to open their stores in about another hour. The restaurants and family taverns were filled with early-morning patrons enjoying breakfast. Everything seemed peaceful. The constable was puzzled. The sergeant had made it sound like all hell was busting loose on the town.

When the chief constable arrived at the station, he understood that the sergeant was right.

The first thing he noticed when he entered the station was the woman. She was beat-up pretty badly. They had her lying on one of the spare cots, and Doc Harrot was already there, treating her wounds.

The next thing the constable noticed was that there was someone sitting behind his desk, in his chair. The man wore a pilot's jacket and a very dirty pair of jeans. He looked like one of the adventurers that lived and worked around the moors.

Sergeant McNetty was standing next to the man, pouring some coffee. A soldier was with the sergeant and another man, dressed in civilian attire but with the posture of a soldier, was standing close by, as well.

Then there was one smallish man, unquestionably a civilian, sitting on a wooden stool in the far right corner. A second man in civvies but with a soldier's stance was standing very close to the little guy, as if he was guarding him.

The scene was totally unexpected for Chief Constable Gardiner. He stood inside the doorway of the police station for a long moment, silently taking in the picture. He almost didn't recognize the office he had been reporting to daily, except Sundays, for the past twenty-seven years.

The man behind the chief's desk saw him first and spoke up. "'Bout time ye got here, Chief. We been waitin' here all mornin'!"

"Get out of my chair!" the chief constable barked. Then he turned toward McNetty. "Sergeant!"

"Chief Constable!"

"What in the blazes of Hades is going on?"

"Sir...I..."

The man in uniform held up a hand, halting the sergeant's prepared excuses. "I'll take this now, Sergeant. Thank you. You have been a great deal of help."

McNetty sighed with real relief and gave the soldier a brief nod of thanks.

Gardiner turned his attention toward the soldier. He spoke with a British accent, stood very straight and proper, and acted as though he had a stiff rod permanently attached to his backside. When he spoke to the chief constable, it was with an air of total authority.

"I am Colonel Lambert of the British Special Air Services. I have been called here by a representative of your government to deal with one Alaister Dyce, a man I am certain you are familiar with. American, uh, investigators, have evidence on Mr. Dyce which proves he is involved in international terrorism, extortion, kidnapping and murder. Therefore, I request your cooperation in capturing and holding Mr. Dyce until the time when we can arrange extradition proceedings and turn Mr. Dyce over to the proper American authorities."

Chief Constable Gardiner put his hands together in front of his chest and looked up at the ceiling. "It's about time and thank God!"

"Your night sergeant has done a wonderful job for us," Colonel Lambert continued. "The man with him behind your desk is a local pilot who assisted the American team."

Cabel gave the chief constable a little wave. "Ye can thank me properly, later, Chief!"

"The woman on the cot who is being attended by your doctor is one of the American team. The rest are still up at Dyce's estate, along with a contingent of American Special Forces. These other two men," Lambert pointed at the two soldiers, "are also members of that team. They are here to protect and escort that man—'' Lambert now pointed at Professor Valentin, sitting in the corner on the stool ''—back to Washington. He is a defected Soviet scientist, the man who Dyce and his people kidnapped. Do you have any questions, Constable?''

Chief Constable Gardiner was more confused than ever. He was about to ask the colonel to repeat the entire story when a thunderous rumble and roaring shook the station house. ''What in the name of the Holy Mother is that?''

The chief constable rushed out of the building and looked around. Other citizens of Inverness were also coming onto the street or poking their heads out of their windows, looking up as the three Royal Navy VH Attack Helicopters armed with U.S. Stinger missiles literally tore the peace of the morning asunder, flying low over the town on a direct northerly course.

''Those are my men,'' said Colonel Lambert, now standing behind the chief constable. ''A full CRW Squadron which will assist the American Special Forces team in the strike on Dyce's estate. It's all over for Mister Alaister Dyce and his terrorist army, Constable. I thought you might like to accompany me on the strike. You could certainly be of some assistance, and I thought you may like to be there at the end of what has probably been a very trying experience for you.''

Chief Constable Gardiner was beaming. ''Aye! Aye! Let me get me hat . . . I'll be with ye!''

The chief constable turned and ran back into the station house, virtually hopping around in his joy and excitement. The British SAS colonel watched him and chuckled. He then looked up at his team, the choppers past the city now, heading north. The fourth assault helicopter was waiting outside of the city and would take him and the constable to Dyce's estate.

The colonel felt good. Months of work were coming to an end. The Americans were probably feeling even better. They had been after Dyce for a year or more. Now, in less than an hour, it would all be over for the techno-terrorist, he thought, and Mr. Alaister Dyce would be feeling the grip of international justice.

GERALD SOUTHWORTH LOWERED the Rangefinder binoculars and gave his head a little shake. The grass beneath him was cold and a bit wet with the early-morning dew.

He, Billy Two and O'Toole were lying on a grassy knoll just west of Dyce's estate, looking down on the grounds. They didn't particularly like what they saw.

The four remaining members of Southworth's Special Forces team were waiting behind them, crouched in the little clearing where Billy had been attending to Lee's wounds. The soldiers were getting a bit restless, wanting to take some action, get the strike going, but Southworth insisted on waiting for the SAS Counter Revolutionary Warfare Squadron he had called in the previous afternoon.

On the knoll, Southworth looked at Billy and O'Toole and spoke softly. "It doesn't look very good for your Colonel Barrabas."

"What do you mean?" Billy Two asked.

"Your colonel is inside the mansion with Alaister Dyce, evidently holding the millionaire hostage. The house is surrounded by Bay and his men. Your people are outnumbered about ten to one.''

Billy Two did something odd. He grinned. "Yes, sir. Obviously Colonel Barrabas has everything exactly the way he wants it.''

Southworth rolled his eyes, then looked back into the binoculars. The British strike force was overdue. They were supposed to arrive at daybreak. The morning shadows were getting a bit short, and Gerald Southworth only hoped that Colonel Barrabas's luck wasn't doing the same!

THE ROW OF FLUORESCENT BULBS gave the basement a garish quality. Barrabas stood at the bottom of the steps and took it all in for a long moment. He was beginning to understand.

The room would have made any tech-nut weep with joy. Rows of computers lined benches and worktables, and were connected with the five satellite dishes in the yard and on the roof of the mansion. Desks and workstations were lit, computer video screens recording data, printers discharging rows of readouts and teletypes clattering incessantly. Barrabas had to admit that he was impressed.

Dyce was actually beaming as he stood in the center of the computer lab. "This is it, Barrabas. My pride and joy!" He waved his hands around, proudly pointing out the massive and complex system like a father introducing his family. "It's a super system, Barrabas...an advanced Kaypro-IV, linked with forty other computers and twenty-five research labs around the world. We've even hacked into twenty U.S. military command posts and the administration's Worldwide Military Command and Control System! We've tapped into everything, Barrabas, every research and development war project the U.S. government has going. We're collecting information on laser and particle beams, automated weapons, military surveillance systems and satellites, killer robots, war in space. Even the Strategic Defense Initiative, or Star Wars! We're connected with government labs and research facilities like the Lawrence Livermore National Laboratory in California. We're tapped into government sponsored research facilities like the labs at the University of Michigan. We're even into half a dozen private corporations with government contracts!"

"So this is it," Barrabas said, still looking around the impressive room. "There is no research and development system . . . no doomsday weapon under design. This is Operation Lightstorm."

Dyce was still beaming. "You have part of it right, Barrabas. The rumors of laser and photon weapons were just propaganda—call them tricks of terrorism. Build a false front of paranoia to keep your government off the track of our real purpose out here. But my computer system is real! And so is the small force of computer hackers and software pirates I've assembled to sort and record all the data we're, uh, borrowing. And so this is very real, Barrabas!"

Dyce stepped over to a large, cluttered desk and lifted a thick report. He waved it around and grinned even wider with his demented pride. "This is a culmination of our many months of work, a report I intend to turn over to the proper representatives of the Soviet Union in a matter of days. This report will give them the leading edge in the race for the militarization of space. I am due in Moscow in two days and I have every intention of turning over this report, and returning Ilya Valentin.''

''Sorry, Dyce. We have Valentin. He's out clear by now, most likely on his way to Washington.''

Dyce continued to grin. ''Doubtful, Barrabas. I have no doubt that Bay's men have found your people and killed them…and our Soviet professor friend is back where he belongs, in my custody! Anyway, it almost doesn't matter. When Moscow has my report and their scientists are able to study what your government has been developing, I shall perform the *coup de résistance*! Operation Lightstorm will really make the Icefort project!''

Barrabas remained silent, waiting for more. Dyce's pride was making the man throw caution to the wind.

Alaister Dyce chuckled. ''I might as well tell you the whole story, Barrabas. After all, my people have you completely surrounded. There is no escape. You are going to die. So I'll give you a little something to think about when you arrive in hell.…

''Lightstorm is a series of viruses. Once the Soviet government has the information to go ahead in the space wars, I'll put a real wrench in the American gears! We're spreading a series of deadly computer viruses into all the systems we've hacked. My computer cowboys are set to enter the damaging data, literally plunging the United States back to square one in the game! That, Colonel Nile Barrabas, is Lightstorm!''

Barrabas smiled. It was time to get out; he had everything he had come for. And he had an excellent way in mind to signal Billy and O'Toole. ''And, this,

Mr. Alaister Dyce, is a Barrabas Storm!'' Barrabas lifted the SMG.

"No!"

Barrabas started at one end of the console and worked his way over the benches and tables covered with computer equipment. When he had made his first pass over the entire system, he started over, sweeping back in the opposite direction.

Dyce's computers were shattered into useless junk. The entire supersystem was blown into pieces by the power of the Heckler & Koch discharging 800 rounds per minute.

When he was done with his destructive sweeps, Barrabas lifted the smoking weapon and gave Dyce his best grin. The room was extremely silent for a long moment, then the pure quiet was completely shattered by the disruption of gunfire. Alaister Dyce had thought he was going to die, but when he removed his hands from his face, he realized he was still alive.

BILLY TWO lifted himself up on extended arms. He heard the automatic fire come from within the mansion, a long series of sweeps and bursts. That must be the colonel's signal!

"It's time to go in!" he said, now turning toward Southworth. Liam O'Toole was already on his feet, set to go.

"Wait!" Gerald Southworth lifted a hand and clutched Billy's sleeve. "The British strikers should be here any minute. We should wait!"

"Sorry," Billy Two said. "The colonel needs us!"

"Gotta go!" O'Toole stated.

The two mercenaries plunged off the knoll and headed back down toward Dyce's estate.

Southworth cursed and looked up toward the skies.

"DAMMIT! I've had enough of this shit!"

Major Bay heard the staccato of the automatic weapon fire come from within the house. His patience was taxed to the very limit. Waiting was no longer of any use. He had to act!

"You men!" He barked instructions to his security force. "Cover the house! Give us fire! If anybody tries to get out, blow them to hell!"

Bay quickly glanced around at his Team-One. They looked as though they, too, had to act to relieve the mounting tension. He smiled for them. "Let's move! Assault and kill!"

Claude Hayes and Alex Nanos were watching from inside the Dyce mansion. Hayes peered through the curtains, then ducked back as the glass shattered and AK fire blew the window apart. The security soldiers were opening up, giving the assault team the cover they needed. He looked over at Nanos. The Greek SOB was positioned at another window.

"Here they come!" Hayes said. "Better go tell the Colonel that the game's on!"

Nanos darted away from his post, ducking as the glass was shattered by automatic fire. The potentially deadly slivers rained down on him, making him crouch to protect his face and neck.

He arrived at the doorway leading down to the basement, where Barrabas and Alaister Dyce were located. "Colonel! Bay and his men are assaulting us!"

Barrabas charged up the steps, shoving Dyce in front of him. He pushed the expatriate into the room and stood next to Nanos, listening. "They're in the house."

Suddenly, as if to accent Barrabas's statement, Hayes yelled as one of the assault team swung through the window from above and leaped on top of the black merc. Hayes was as ready for the attack as he could be, taking the fall with a roll, getting clear of the other man and defending himself with a blocking arm. The Tanto knife cut into his flesh, making him wince with the sudden pain. He reached out with his good arm and grabbed the killer's knife hand and pushed his weight against the resisting fighter. They rolled, and Hayes's superior strength carried him over. With the Team-One killer now on his back, they struggled in a deadly hand-to-hand.

Nanos was about to rush over and help when two more of the assault team came around the corner to his left.

"Behind you!" Barrabas ducked into the staircase to the basement laboratory as rounds from the killers' MAC-10s tore up the wall next to him.

Nanos ducked, dove forward and rolled behind the cover of a thick, plush chair. The MAC-10 fire ripped into the carpet and the expensive upholstery of the chair. Nanos moved quickly, coming up as soon as he was behind the cover, returning fire with his Heckler & Koch. He caught his attacker with a full burst in the chest. The man's body was thrown backward and hit the floor with a solid thump.

Alaister Dyce had crawled under a table and was cowering, completely terrified to be caught in the cross fire. He pressed his shaking body against the thick carpet, at the breaking point with grief and fear.

Barrabas waited inside the doorway at the top of the stairs that led down to the basement. Bay's killer worked his way along the wall, thinking Barrabas had returned to the basement. He was careless, believing he had the mercenary colonel trapped downstairs.

Suddenly the situation changed. Barrabas moved, his strong hand darting out in a flash, grasping the man's jacket and pulling him off balance, tumbling him down the stairs. Barrabas swung around and discharged a short burst from his SMG into the back of the falling man's head. The attacker was dead before he hit the basement floor.

Barrabas stepped back into the room and turned his attention to his men. Nanos gave him a little wave; he was okay. Hayes was still on the floor in a battle of strength with his assailant.

Barrabas was about to jump over and lend a hand to the black merc when Hayes gave a mighty push downward, using all his remaining strength and body weight. The Tanto survival knife twisted and plunged, going into the soft flesh of the attacker's belly.

The man gasped in pain, knowing he was as good as dead. Hayes stood, picked up the SMG from where he had set it in the battle and gave the writhing killer a quick burst to finish the job.

"Claude?"

Hayes turned to Barrabas and grinned. "I'm fine, Colonel!"

"We have to get moving…make our way to the rear and meet Billy and O'Toole at the escape route."

Nanos and Hayes were ready to join Barrabas and follow him out of the house when the main assault of the attacking team hit them.

"Colonel!"

Nanos pointed behind Barrabas, then immediately dove back to cover behind the torn chair as MAC-10 fire filled the room. Three new attackers were charging into the room from the back. Barrabas also ducked and rolled to cover behind the sofa. The window behind him burst with a loud crash and a Bay shock trooper leaped on top of him. They were swinging into the other windows of the room also, two catching Hayes from behind as he stared at the colonel's predicament. The room had become filled with Bay's Team-One killers.

The chair Nanos was using for cover was being torn to shreds by the constant barrage of automatic fire. Rounds were cutting their way through, one catching him in the meat of his shoulder, biting hard. He winced and cursed and looked at his fellow soldiers, struggling, engaged in deadly hand-to-hand combat, fighting for their lives. And the assaulters continued to pour into the room.

Alex Nanos would never really understand why he did what he did next. It could have been instinct for survival, or a death wish by fire that so many professional soldiers had. He didn't have time to think about it at the moment. His three attackers were moving up on him, sweeping the room, advancing quickly. He couldn't return fire. He was pinned down under the superior firepower, and the enemy was making a steady, relentless drive.

And Alex Nanos got mad! He was tired of fighting these rat-trappers with their hit-and-run methods. The cowards, he raged, as he was overcome by unreasoning, incautious fury. He cursed all the gods with one mighty battle cry, pulled his last Mk grenade off the web, pulled the pin, counted to five and threw it into the center of the room.

"Use this to play ball, you sons of bitches!"

"Grenade—" Two of the killers shouted it. The other was too stunned to speak.

Nanos dove to the floor and pulled an armchair on top of him to give him cover against the shock of the explosion. Hayes rolled with the man he was fighting, maneuvering the other's body as a type of shield, using the very last of his strength to hold the man in front of him. Barrabas just went limp, allowing the two men trying to tear him apart with bayonets to lurch on top of him. Then the room was filled with white light and the subsequent concussion that made their heads throb and feel as if they were about to burst, and then came the heat and fire and shattering of the world around them. A hundred things broke and burst and flew wildly apart at once, filling the huge sitting room with deadly projectiles. And somewhere, inside all the chaos and havoc, men were screaming.

Then it was all over within a few seconds, and there was thick silence. There was smoke and the terrible burning stench permeating the atmosphere. A few things were still breaking, falling with the slight aftershocks. Glass crumbled, mixing with the soft moans of men wounded or dying.

There was some slight movement, rustling, broken things crunching as weight was being shifted.

"Alex?"

"Yeah."

Barrabas crawled out from under the pile of dead bodies that had shielded him. "Alex...are you okay?"

Nanos pushed what was left of the chair off him and knelt in the rubble. "Huh? Can't hear you, Colonel. My ears are ringin'."

Claude Hayes rolled over and got up on his hands and knees. He shook his head, trying to clear it. Blood was dripping from his nose and running out of his left ear. "Nanos! Christ! You crazy Greek bastard! Are you tryin' to kill us?"

"Listen!"

Barrabas stood up on shaky legs and walked over to look out one of the broken windows. The assault team had arrived from Inverness. The British RN helicopters were sweeping in from the south, low, powerful and menacing. Another band of rescuers was coming through the main gate. They moved like a highly trained, elite unit, possibly American Special Forces. They were being led by Billy Two and O'Toole.

Barrabas watched the action for a moment. The choppers were sweeping the grounds, the men inside returning fire as a few of Bay's remaining security forces put up a meager fight. One of the copters hovered over the carriage house, where a number of vehicles were parked. Some of Bay's soldiers were trying to escape. The chopper fired a single Stinger missile into the garage and blew it into useless rubble and flame. A few of the mercenaries survived the initial eruption and lurched back into the yard, with their clothes set afire.

Barrabas stepped back from the window and leaned his weight against the wall. Hayes was standing next to him now.

"Should we go out and assist in the attack, sir?" the black merc asked.

Barrabas felt like smiling, but it hurt too much. He was so filled with pride that it made his eyes water. He wiped some running blood off his chin, put a friendly hand on Hayes's shaking shoulder and forced a grin. "No, Claude, I think we'll sit this one out . . ."

IT DIDN'T TAKE LONG for the SAS attack squadron and the SF team to finish the job. The sheer power of their attack and overwhelmingly superior training and firepower gave them the edge from the start.

Major Bay saw his world coming apart around him. His Team-One had been blown to smithereens inside the mansion. A British SAS squadron was coming down on his broken army like a storm from hell. He stood alone at the back of the huge, smoking house, having just directed his best men to their deaths, and decided his best plan of action was to make a run for it.

Bay turned around to bolt and came face-to-face with Billy Starfoot II and Liam O'Toole.

"Going somewhere, Major?" Billy asked.

Bay looked around desperately, seeking an escape route. There was no place to go, nowhere to run this time. He was trapped.

Liam O'Toole lifted his SMG and aimed it point-blank at Bay's head. "Try it, Major. I owe you big!"

"Easy, soldier." Gerald Southworth and two Special Forces warriors came up behind the two mercs. "The major will pay for his crimes. We want him back in Washington."

O'Toole reluctantly lowered his weapon. "Sir..."

Chief Constable Gardiner stood in the center of the yard in front of the smoking Dyce mansion. A huge, billowing black cloud was rising up from the once majestic Elizabethan home, fouling the blue Scottish sky. The reign of Alaister Dyce was at a fiery end.

The constable gave a start as there was a sudden movement in the front of the house. What was left of the front door was opening, and a man was stepping out. He was followed by others, three in all.

"Colonel!" Gardiner called to the SAS squadron leader. "Colonel Lambert! Come here! Quickly!"

Lambert was busy directing a squad of his commandos flushing out a pocket of resisters in a distant south corner of the estate grounds. It wouldn't take long for the SAS warriors to take out the band of defenders.

Lambert heard the chief constable calling and ran back to the front yard. "What is it, Constable?"

Staggering out of the mansion were four of the most wretched-looking individuals the colonel had ever seen. They were bleeding from dozens of small wounds and cuts, and their clothes were torn to virtual rags. Three of them were carrying Heckler & Koch SMGs, pointing them at the fourth man. He was Alaister Dyce.

The little group of survivors walked up to Colonel Lambert. He and Constable Gardiner were standing in stunned silence.

The big man in the lead spoke. "I am Colonel Nile Barrabas." He gave Lambert a shaky salute.

"Good Lord!" said the SAS colonel. "You men must have been through hell in there! God! Let us help you...medic!"

Gerald Southworth, his two Special Forces soldiers, Billy Two and Liam O'Toole paraded over to join the little band in the center of the yard. They had a hapless and conquered Major Bay with them.

Southworth approached Barrabas. "Colonel Barrabas. It is indeed a pleasure to be able to meet you. We thought you were dead."

"Not this time," Barrabas said. "Somebody back in Washington must think we're pretty important to send you out here."

"Well, it wasn't you, exactly, Colonel. The President was concerned about Ilya Valentin. He is safely on his way back to the U.S. by now, Colonel. Thank you. You and your men have done a splendid job. I wish there was some way to show our appreciation, but...well, you know...all this didn't really happen."

Barrabas nodded slightly. "Yeah. Whatever..."

He was staring at one of Southworth's men, a sergeant standing guard next to Major Bay. There was something about the man, but he couldn't put his finger on it. He was too tired to rack his brain so he dismissed the vague sense of premonition.

"We're going to get you and your men some medical attention, now, Colonel," said Lambert. "Please let us take over the situation and go with my man..."

Barrabas extended his hand wearily, and the two men shook hands.

Billy Two was standing next to Hayes, grinning at him.

"Claude! You look pretty bad!"

The black mercenary just glared at the Osage. Nanos spoke up. "It took you some while to come back for us. But it worked out, so we forgive you!" Chortling, they slapped each other on the back and shoulder, pleased to be alive and to have completed the mission.

Two SAS raiders led Barrabas and the wounded SOBs to a makeshift medic station. Gerald Southworth watched them limp away, shaking his head slightly and thinking that they were the best damned warriors he had ever known. And woman, he thought as he remembered Dr. Hatton. He turned his attention back to Alaister Dyce and Major Bay.

Dyce also needed medical attention. He had taken the grenade explosion from his hiding place under the antique table.

Southworth turned toward his men. "Sergeant Hudson."

"Sir!" Hudson stepped forward.

"Take these prisoners to one of the choppers. See to it that Mister Dyce gets the proper medical attention."

"Sir." Hudson and the other SF soldier led the two international criminals away.

The battle of the Dyce estate was completely over. All resistance had been thwarted. The remaining security soldiers had been killed or captured.

Southworth and Colonel Lambert walked over to the spot where Barrabas and his men were receiving attention.

Barrabas looked up and asked, "Where are Dyce and Bay?"

"I had Sergeant Hudson take them—"

"Sergeant Hudson? *No!*" Barrabas lurched to his feet and began to run as fast as he could when he heard a series of explosions.

Barrabas and the raiders ran to the clearing next to the estate where the Royal Navy choppers had landed. Three of the copters were in flames, blown apart by U.S. M-26 grenades. The fourth was revving up, about to take off, with Alaister Dyce and Major Bay on board and Hudson desperately trying to make it to the helicopter before takeoff.

Along with Barrabas, Southworth, Lambert and a dozen of the raiders ran after the lifting chopper, but it swept north, away from them.

Sergeant Hudson stood in the center of the disrupted landing zone. His SF partner was lying next to him, dead, shot in the chest with Hudson's M-16. The sergeant gritted his teeth and lifted his smoking weapon toward the men rushing at him but before he could fire, Barrabas got him with a head shot.

Southworth ran over and stood by the dead Special Forces sergeant. Liam O'Toole walked up from the back and just calmly looked after the helicopter, then lifted his fingers in a victory salute.

The NSA agent was totally confused by the astounding events. "What the bloody hell . . . ?"

O'Toole started counting. "Three . . . two . . . one!"

The fleeing chopper was away from the grounds by now, moving quickly. It suddenly lurched and the first Mk grenade blew the chopper into flames and billowing smoke. The second erupted, finishing the job, sending debris through the sky. In a split second, all that remained was a lingering ball of phantom flames and the rudders plummeting toward the moor.

Now O'Toole was giving Southworth a conspiratorial look. "I managed to give them a couple of presents before they took off—something I thought they'd get a bang out of..."

Southworth just shook his head. He looked back down at the dead Special Forces soldier at his feet. Barrabas stepped up next to him and spoke softly. "Sorry, Jerry. There's your mole."

"Hudson?"

"His face seemed familiar, but I was tired and couldn't place him right away. He was at the gym where Jessup gave me the initial briefing on the kidnapped Professor Valentin. He was posing as a bodybuilder. He obviously overheard our discussion and reported to Bay. That explains why I've been hounded by the major's killer teams since the beginning. It's also how the kill squads had American weapons, and how Carter was hired to assassinate Isaac in Berlin."

Southworth was frowning and appeared to be deep in thought. "Of course. Hudson told Carter he was acting on orders from my office."

"Yes. And that's why Carter thought he and I were working for the same source. He thought he had been hired by the NSA."

"Damn!" Southworth looked up and stared into the empty sky. All that remained of the escape chopper was a trace of smoke. "I wonder why he did it."

Barrabas shrugged. "Probably greed." He holstered his Browning and walked away.

Southworth stood by himself for a long moment, then forced himself out of his blue mood. He looked around as the professional assault team went about the task of finishing their business. The mission had been a total success.

Southworth saw Barrabas standing alone in the distance, looking aloof and somewhat forlorn. He walked over and put a hand on the mercenary colonel's shoulder. "Don't be so glum, Barrabas. The mission was a smashing success. We have Ilya Valentin back and that should put a crimp in the Icefort project. Dyce and Bay's entire operation has been blown to smithereens...and Operation Lightstorm with them. And we found the mole that's been making my life hell for the past month. Not a bad job, if I do say so myself!"

Barrabas still had a pensive expression. He was looking down at a dead security soldier. It was the young French Army soldier he had talked to in the bar in Paris. He hadn't listened.

Barrabas felt worn out. Maybe it was time to take stock.

He looked at Southworth. "Do you think God has a sense of humor, Jerry?"

"What...?"

Barrabas looked very tired, but he said, "I mean, would he understand the Barrabas code? I've always acted on that," he added as if to clarify a point. He gave the NSA agent a last salute before he turned and walked away.

by GAR WILSON

The battle-hardened five-man
commando unit known as Phoenix
Force continues its onslaught
against the hard realities of global
terrorism in an endless crusade for
freedom, justice and the rights of
the individual. Schooled in guerrilla
warfare, equipped with the latest in
lethal weapons, Phoenix Force's
adventures have made them a
legend in their own time. Phoenix
Force is the free world's foreign
legion!

"Gar Wilson is excellent! Raw action
attacks the reader on every page."
—Don Pendleton

Phoenix Force titles are available
wherever paperbacks are sold.

PHOENIX FORCE

GOLD
EAGLE

TAKE 'EM NOW

FOLDING SUNGLASSES
FROM GOLD EAGLE

Mean up your act with these tough, street-smart shades. Practical, too, because they fold 3 times into a handy, zip-up polyurethane pouch that fits neatly into your pocket. Rugged metal frame. Scratch-resistant acrylic lenses. Best of all, they can be yours for only $6.99.

MAIL YOUR ORDER TODAY.

Send your name, address, and zip code, along with a check or money order for just $6.99 + .75¢ for postage and handling (for a total of $7.74) payable to Gold Eagle Reader Service. (New York and Iowa residents please add applicable sales tax.)

Remove from pouch.

unfold once.

unfold twice.

and they're ready to wear

Gold Eagle Reader Service
901 Fuhrmann Blvd.
P.O. Box 1396
Buffalo, N.Y. 14240-1396

GES-1A

Offer not available in Canada.